James Mason and the Walk-in Closet

Also by June Akers Seese

What Waiting Really Means

Is This What Other Women Feel Too?

June Akers Seese

James Mason and the Walk-in Closet

Dalkey Archive Press

The title novella and "Near Ocasions of Sin" are published here for the first time; the other stories originally appeared in the *Carolina Quarterly, Catalyst, Lullwater Review, South Carolina Review,* and *Witness.*

ISBN 1-56478-040-6

Partially funded by grants from the National Endowment for the Arts and the Illinois Arts Council.

Dalkey Archive Press
4241 Illinois State University
Normal, IL 61790-4241

Printed on permanent/durable acid-free paper and bound in the United States of America.

Contents

Acknowledgments

I would like to thank Jean and David Bergmark and Michael Maher as well as Orla McCurtain of the Irish Tourist Board. My thanks also go to Ann Raney Davis, and I dedicate this book to her. I would be remiss if I did not include Zaron W. Burnett, Jr., and Lawrence Koltonow; and, once again, Pearl Cleage, my friend to the grave.

James Mason and the Walk-in Closet

1

Some people say my friend Lucy talks like Jackie O. Granted Lucy works at an art gallery and speaks in a whisper to the customers. Granted Jackie's voice is soft, and she made that tour through the White House to explain the paintings; but Lucy doesn't look anything like Jackie Onassis, so it's hard to see why they say it and harder still to see why Lucy repeats it.

Lucy grew up in Manhattan and went to school there, too, close to home. She didn't think of leaving the city until her mother moved to Scottsdale. All those years of smoking, and her mother's doctor quoted statistics as if they were bullets. Lucy called it a death sentence.

Scottsdale has the most beautiful flowers I have ever seen; yet the gallery where Lucy works has a two-foot cactus at the door. Indian rugs on the walls and a silver teapot beside the phone. There's no shortage of tea these days, and we drink Irish Breakfast. Last year I brought Lucy a lifetime supply along with a crystal pitcher from the Shannon Airport. I had spent the winter in Dublin living with a man called Cookie. Now I'm staying around the corner from the gallery in one room with a walk-in closet. It seems to be enough.

Lucy met my plane again today. This time it was a week in Mexico City, and I had Spanish lace in my hand. Lucy took it and told me what little I'd missed while I was away. Her mother is all taken up with her newest lover. He's ten years younger and launching a business in vintage clothing.

I try to return the conversation to faraway places, the farther the better. Lucy has accumulated enough vacation time to ease herself into the heat down there where loose clothes and siestas make life bearable. So far, she refuses to fly to Mexico, or anywhere else for that matter.

As for me, I know Lucy's story by heart. She repeats herself like an old woman—prefacing each revision with an admonition to stop her if—but there's no stopping Lucy. Her soft voice grows softer once the first phrase leaves her mouth, and I strain to catch the final syllables.

My friend has a mother who taught her to see the brightness of a flower and give directions to a servant. Lucy can't remember what she did or where she went before the first day of school; but every day, from that time on, her mother took a cab to Rattner's where Lucy chose her heart's desire, a thick, spongy cake that had no name.

Lucy still loves bright colors. Her stroller, which was kept for her brother, had three yellow buttons on a steel pole. She rubbed them every afternoon, as if they were magic, while the nurse held her brother and his formula in a stiff embrace. The nurse's cap and long skirts stayed outside the rules of fashion, but her mother's clothes were cast aside as the seasons changed.

They were peaceful children, and Lucy still thinks she had an easy life. After school no one came to interfere with their hot chocolate and French pastries. Steam rose from the boiled milk and clouded their eyes. Lucy's brother had a tic, and she watched his eye open and close faster than any wink. They were never apart.

There were no pictures in Lucy's apartment, so her mother left the two children in art museums on the maid's day off. There they were protected by guards with shiny buttons and fortified with Cadbury bars in the pockets of their coats. In my mind's eye, I see Lucy and her brother sitting upright on soft leather benches savoring the chocolate squares and whispering to each other.

Lucy's mother hated snow and strangers, so Lucy and her brother watched the streets from their apartment windows and told each other fairy tales. In the library,

Lucy nibbled peppermint wafers, learning their pastel flavors. Lemon was her favorite. She learned to walk slowly, and she never tipped anything over. Candy dishes were everywhere.

In the summers the family moved to the White Mountains in New Hampshire where they played croquet and drank lemonade. The grass was green and safely fenced. Lucy learned the name of every wildflower and the big books they came in. Her father stayed in the city, but he called every afternoon. The maid told him Lucy was happy and her mother was asleep.

Little by little, Lucy lifted her secrets up for my scrutiny: she picked her nose and put the crusts under table-tops where no one could find them. Thick, jungle growth. Rough and dry. She peed in the bathwater and felt the yellowing bubbles grow cold and leave the tub. Then she rubbed herself to sleep bunched up in her thin cotton gown. In the middle of the night, she walked through the bedrooms checking the breathing of her mother and the maid huddled in their twin beds under old summer blankets. Unable to leave, she finished out the night on the floor outside their door without a pillow or a sheet.

In the morning, the maid brought a tray to Lucy's room and then found Lucy and brought her back too. A yellow rose mashed in oatmeal, its thorns thick and flat. Lucy removed the petals and slid the oatmeal into the toilet. Her bedside copy of *Cinderella* was hunter green, and the three sisters were drawn in silhouettes. No matter how many times she read the story, Lucy could never see why anyone could be so wicked.

Life wasn't all pastry trays and tidy afternoons. Her mother didn't like it when the children were sick and couldn't eat her sweets. She brought them anyway, and they sat untouched on the nightstands of their sick-rooms, the crinkled papers they came in fluttering in the air of the heat vent. They had to content themselves with the hum of the vaporizer and the bright red nail polish on the maid's fingernails.

Lucy's brother died before they had a chance to leave

home together. It was an accident. His glasses fell off and when he bent over to retrieve them, he tumbled down the stairs. He never even cried. Lucy still has a picture of him. He's sitting in the metal stroller, and she is kneeling beside him, her fingers mashing the yellow buttons. Their mother stands behind the stroller, smiling. It is July, and the willow tree is bent to the ground.

2

Beauty is a blessing and a curse. And Lucille is outside the fray. Sitting in the Tate Gallery with her carefully filed fingernails and big watch, she can modulate the history of a painting so it leaves the cool walls and meets my eyes in that light that hangs around for a while on summer afternoons. She knows the artists and their tools, and no name is too long for her to remember.

For five years, she has called Las Vegas to report her cash receipts to the crook who owns the gallery. Lucille uncrates the boxes, polishes those little brass lights above the paintings, and waits behind her glass table, seven days a week, from ten to six, as if it mattered.

We both live close to the gallery. Lucille's Victorian house, the only one in Old Town, is green—inside and out. The woman who waters her grass and putters around in the flowers is as regular as the clock in Lucille's entry— the only thing of hers I covet—pure glass, and the pendulum looks as if it floats in the air.

Lucille was sick last winter with phlebitis, so she bought footstools—one for work and two for home—and there is no living room more comfortable. The cushions on her sofa feel like a feather bed.

On summer nights, we sit with our laps full of travel books and spiral dictionaries. We gossip and listen to the radio. Somebody died in the desert last week. The heat wave is expected to continue. We never miss the eleven o'clock news.

When I'm home in bed, I have time to think about

Lucille. I have been trying to drag her with me to the real desert for a long time, but she is satisfied with Georgia O'Keeffe's bones and sand. Our plans stay on paper, and I go off alone.

I was leafing through a book of photographs the other night, and I came across Diane Arbus and her camera. "Freaks are born aristocrats, of the spirit," she claims, "because they have already passed the test." Ready-made suffering. Maybe that explains my feelings for Lucille. She wasn't born a freak, but she had become one when I met her. Massive and hidden. All you have to do is be with her mother for three minutes to realize the pull of fate: "Lucille, I have a present for you." That woman will never have anything to give anyone. There are some things that can't be changed. And that's as much philosophy as I want to bother with at this ungodly hour of the morning.

It's not that I'm reduced to the classifieds, but I did go off to Ireland, and I will have to find another job. Lying takes preparation. Numbers. Months. The right expression on your face. No boss likes to think you are going to bolt. Their jobs mean a lot, to them! I am a receptionist. Another college girl who paid the price of reading what I wanted for four years.

I move around on my trips, so it is a relief to come home to air that doesn't destroy me. Scottsdale is dry and predictable. Mildew and moths are on nobody's mind here. My clothes are as safe as my respiratory system, but it wasn't always that way.

I grew up in Detroit on the East Side. Polish bakeries and Dodge Main and air I couldn't breathe. My parents had an answer for everything, and my sister bought it all. Getting pregnant was just a little sidestep in the polka. So was her husband's religion. They still ate pierogies in the dining room after their wedding, and he made friends with the priest. We drank all night and moved the folding chairs onto the back porch when the sun came up, hot.

I would have bled to death to get away. All that color— red nail polish we used in those days, the red checks on our themes at Sacred Heart High School, my red corduroy jumper—chased a crazy zigzag through my head as I stared at my mother's dead garden and thought about the little frog and all that bright red blood. Abortion was illegal in 1972, and that waiting room had neither Kleenex nor magazines.

A butcher on Dexter. I sat with those giant sanitary napkins and a bottle of Darvon and cried because I couldn't tell anybody. Finally I got up and went to the movies. I saw everything close to the Fox. Darkness helped. The lights blurred, and the staircases and carpets seemed like a cave. Then I went home and slept in a puddle of blood. I was afraid to call the doctor, if that's what he was. I didn't feel dirty, I felt my dreams had drained away my heart, and it would be lying somewhere on the floor when I finally got up—looking like a glossy picture from a medical book—all blood and muscle and torn out. I stuffed the sheets in the trash and thrashed around on the stained mattress the rest of the summer alone.

That was the summer I read Kafka and planned to go to the Newport Jazz Festival but didn't. I boiled two eggs every morning and took one with me for lunch. I couldn't look at meat.

One day a man from Pakistan had a fit in the office on the other side of the counter. He was working on a Ph.D. and Admissions had lost his transcripts. It was the appropriate response, and we were pulled into his rage. The office was full of incompetents who stayed out for lunch and didn't know the alphabet.

Near the end of August, I lost my umbrella and was walking home with my hair and dress soaking wet when a man pulled over and offered me a lift. "I don't know why I'm doing this," he said. "Your whole department has ruined my life."

He had a brogue, and I trusted him. He taught Irish poetry and was reading for his orals and working on his dissertation. I didn't type it. He didn't take over that much. I lay in his arms and looked out my open window.

I told him everything. "I don't think I can ever make love again."

He made it all into a joke: "Well, I have patience," he laughed. "If I can survive that madhouse you call an office without kicking in the file cabinets, I can wait for you. My family grays early—see if you can hurry it up."

A week went by. In the evenings, I watched him type. The Irishman's dissertation was on *Finnegans Wake.* My girlfriends had all read D. H. Lawrence for the sex scenes, and I moved along in that direction for a while.

"There are other ways to make love. Lady Chatterley didn't know about them, but the upper classes needn't concern us!" We were in the middle of chicken noodle soup, and it was raining. I took a few days off work.

Why can't romance like that last? He was so funny and civilized. We agreed not to spoil it with marriage.

Mostly we stayed home or took walks. He didn't know anyone outside the English Department, and the summer school teachers went their separate ways. I had a lot of people I wanted to avoid. My sister called me once in a while to tell me about her breathing classes: "I bought a bottle of Mother's Friend to put on my stomach."

"Don't get carried away!"

"You have to think about the future. Stretch marks show in a bikini."

"My sister is never going to get a scholarship!" The Irishman smiled.

Fall arrived too fast. He passed his orals and turned in his dissertation. We went to the library to listen to recordings of *Finnegans Wake.*

"You better talk this one over with your cronies. I'm in over my head!" He kissed me in front of that miserable librarian who spies in the cubicles. We walked down the marble steps and passed the dwarfed cherry trees.

The week before Christmas, he died. A car wreck. An out-of-towner got confused on the freeway. My sister came to the funeral with her mouth shut and head covered. We made quite a pair. She, eight months pregnant, and me, six inches taller and too thin.

I just didn't know what to think or what to do, so I followed the crowd that year. My presents were wrapped, and I sent a few cards. The last one was to his mother in Dublin. It's a poor city, and the statues and pubs are not much consolation. I bought myself an album by Richard Dyer-Bennett. He's an Irish tenor, and those pure high notes cleared my head.

I kept my job, but things were quiet after the new semester got underway. It gets dark early in Detroit, and I settled in to the reading I had planned for the winter. Modern Library had just brought out a collection of Henry James. *Portrait of a Lady* has a good ending. Isabel Archer picks up things and goes right on.

3

I'll tell you all I know. Little things. What Lucy hid. A narrow box of thin mints in her bathroom and four more at the gallery. I could smell them, once I knew. Some suggestions were made. "Get away." Those hideaways where the rich pay two thousand dollars a week to dine on lettuce leaves and plain yogurt and pretend all day, by a pool. Glossy brochures at the gallery and in the baskets at her house. Lucy threw them out, but they kept coming. The chambers of commerce of every city in Europe knew Lucy's size.

Invitations to Sunday dinners, catered, were the flip side of the coin. Greasy cheese-filled dishes; sharp, salty Chinese sauces; an ever-present mason jar of candied fruit—all part of a silent picture. No earphones or historical perspective. No docent. Mother and daughter were masters of the unspoken. An art, too.

Labor Day weekend, Lucy's mother suggested a picnic at Tailsen. Her lover was away on business. I refused. Lucy hates nature in the raw as much as I do. The low bushes are part of a dead green landscape where only the heat is alive. Tailsen is a disappointment every tourist must see. Ugly rocks set in concrete and little sticks trying to look modern, in crazy arrangements, on what appears to be a roof. I have never gone inside.

Lucy packed a hamper. Pickles and ham roll-ups. Club soda and Chardonnay. Royal blue cloth napkins and mangoes. Tiny knives to peel them with, and multicolored plastic plates to lay them on. A candle to keep the bugs away.

The Sunday before the outing, her mother kept harping on purple sunsets and Camel Back Mountain until Lucy registered a protest: "You'll spoil it with all this preliminary description, Mother!"

The mountain looks like a three-part dung heap, and who can appreciate the sky when sweat is pouring off your body and your back aches? Who can appreciate a stony landscape with three hundred pounds pressing against your bones? Where every step counts too much? Blood can run hot as well as cold.

It was a record day for tourists at Tailsen, and warm enough to scramble eggs in the gravel.

Lucy smashed her mother's face with a rock and drove away.

The highway is flat once you leave the gravel incline.

Boring.

Dead.

The hamper was still there, untouched, the next morning. Lucy opened the gallery at ten. She was arrested with a cup of coffee in her hand. Journalists out here are big on human interest details. She was wearing silver hoop earrings.

I can't believe Lucy planned it. What did that woman say to her? The last words! What were they? Fat people learn to take jokes. I know it wasn't a joke.

Kate Smith was fat and dignified, like Lucy seemed to be. Look at Orson Welles. They hid their bodies under long sleeves and baggy gabardine. They gave up quietly. Intelligence and talent have many uses. Don't tell me they weren't just as angry!

The funeral was short. The coffin closed. The preacher had false teeth, and he convinced us the Lord is his shepherd. Lucy stayed in her cell. The coffin was *not* a cheap pine box. Donations were sent to some foundation for childhood asthma in Phoenix, and the room smelled of cinnamon air freshener.

I went home and called my sister.

"What got into you?" she began after the operator announced how long the distance was. She likes to delude herself into thinking I'm cheap.

There was too much static on the line for her to hear me. "Go to hell," I said, and hung up.

4

The week Lucille left for the state prison, I rented a VCR and watched James Mason movies. Every morning I boiled an egg and buttered a slice of pumpernickel and carried it to my bed, where I stayed all day with the shades drawn and the air conditioner on "freeze." I can't make friends with Mason. He's gone too. What was I looking for?

In the movies, you can go back to the beginning, again and again. James Mason needn't stay bent and balding. I can find him ramrod-straight, with a shock of black hair over one eye—all in the same day. I can hear him affect a German accent and watch his leather boots move forward before my nap; then see him pour whiskey for Charlotte Rampling with his puffy liver-spotted hands when I wake up. His upper lip still thin. His teeth still crooked. From *The Desert Fox* to *The Verdict,* he remains the prince of fucking darkness.

His final movie interests me most. In it, he plays lord of the manor—detached, thoughtful, in full command of the voice that makes my heart stop. He was seventy-five years old when the movie was filmed in England, and he died a few months later. It's called *The Shooting Party.* The characters, gathered for a weekend of talk and competition, seem to know what's coming and who they are. Of course, nobody knows, and they are felled by chance, too. But, for two hours, the illusion lasts.

Then it's over, and I walk out of the theater, smashed up against the facts: Mason's dead, Great Britain has collapsed, the manor houses are bed-and-breakfasts for the least of us, and Brixton riots soil the city.

From 1913 to 1984, and back to bed. *A Star Is Born* is like a toddy. Mason's silk pajamas and "a new world" of celluloid. But these illusions fade, too, into real dreams: jail cells at the state prison that don't fit Lucille—and her trial which had no verdict, only a sentence.

I haven't seen her since the murder. I followed the trial on TV and saw the artist's drawings of the judge and the jury and her. She looks better in caricature.

The gallery is closed now, and Lucille has sold her house to pay the attorneys. How can anyone think she will ever be rid of her mother? Or that she was not in prison all along? Cremation may have burned away the bruises, but that's all it did.

I write. Lucille answers. The ceiling fan gathers dust, and the phone never rings.

Dear Lucille,
    I don't feel sorry for you, and sometimes I envy your clear-cut life. I have been rereading *The Trial* since you went away. You know what you did and why you're there. More than I can say for Kafka's hero.
    I killed something, too. It was a long time ago. I had to get rid of part of me and someone else. A blood clot. Is this how you felt about your mother?
                                                    Mary Ben

Mary Ben,
    What makes you think any of that applies to me?
                                                    Lucy

It was a short correspondence—six weeks—six letters, and then Lucille died in her sleep. That's how the news-caster put it. He made it seem natural. And it was. What is more natural than a heart that wears down under all that weight?

I'm trying to decide what to do. Today, James Mason was old again, riding along with Sherlock Holmes in misty gray-green air, searching for Jack the Ripper. The carriage wheels roll over the cobblestones. Mason's hat is high.

5

I got to a point where James Mason didn't help. When the sheets got too sweaty, even for me. I got up and surveyed my closet. The hangers were jammed together, and panty hose covered the floor. Tired from all the possibilities, I ran a shower and let the hot water hit my back until it turned cold. All afternoon I sat on the bed, skimming a stack of *Time* magazines to see what had been happening in the world since I drew the shades. The terrorists are still at it, and Hollywood PR has not let up.

I keep a few photographs on my nightstand: the Irishman, my sister's girls, and my uncle. He is standing straight, in a white shirt open at the throat. A cigarette in his mouth, flanked by his brothers, he appears invincible. The picture frame is sterling silver, polished.

My uncle, a bachelor, was the voice of reason in our family until he was overtaken by age a few years ago, the youngest and smartest brother, the one who loaned me two hundred fifty dollars with no strings attached, the summer I met the Irishman. A tall man, my uncle, with a commanding step, he moved beyond ethnic issues and two-bit religiosity into a place the rest of our family couldn't touch. Protected by money and brains, he could afford to stay put. I couldn't.

Suddenly, the February I finished the Henry James novels, all those diseases the pamphlets warn against were his. His heart. His blood pressure. His lungs. Then came another funeral and my inheritance. My sister was furious this time, but what could she do? They played "Amazing Grace" and she picked at her hangnails and mumbled something about protocol. Not that she used the word. She never understood words or my uncle or Protestant hymns or priests, for that matter. She certainly didn't understand how I ended up with all that money and she had to be satisfied with a Buick convertible with a broken taillight.

I traveled around the country looking for a little freedom. The cities were a diversion. Their streets pulled me forward. The hills and narrow sidewalks met the thick soles of my shoes, and I had the illusion of movement. My uncle would have approved. He stayed away from flat and easy paths, himself. My father told me when you need money you find out who your friends are. My uncle will always be my best friend.

6

If I had told Lucille the truth about my winter in Dublin, she would have laughed at me. Besides, the truth will rarely get you anywhere. You must see it to survive, and after that it's all subterfuge. Lucille swallowed my story about the Irish revolution in the North and gunfire and my squeamishness. She didn't know much about geography! She never looked beyond the seductive voice (on tape) and slow-building words of the Irishman's younger brother, Cookie Reddington. A dutiful correspondent. Gallant with me, his errant brother's leftover woman. Cookie hung around the fringes of the Abbey Players, doing his best acting job in a leather jacket and tight pants, holding his cigarette in the European manner, cutting his meat the same way—trying to make his manhood appear unquestionable.

All last winter, he was a tidy roommate and easy companion. I don't mind being used as a cover-up, so it was back to Cookie I went, after a rainy weekend in Seattle, expecting more of the same. I bought a yellow slicker and cleared up the rest of my business by phone. I also bought a pair of cheap rubber boots and some warm underwear. It felt good to be outside again, after all those

days in bed with James Mason. I thought about him in
Lolita. Didn't Humbert Humbert flee through motel rooms
and drenched parking lots as they crossed the country in
that white station wagon? I felt close to Humbert. Wasn't
I going back to Ireland to uncertain lodgings and youth?
Like Humbert, I craved one person, alone, locked away
from the pretenders.

7

The plane left the ground, and the little light above my
head cut off. James Mason's voice went to Dublin with
me. I sat next to a tremulous grandmother who talked
about geraniums and showed me her daughter's wedding picture. I nodded here and there, but just inside my
eyelids, Mason's wide fingers stuffed cotton between
Lolita's toes. Sensuality at its most unnerving moment.
Captured!

We changed planes in New York, but it was Shannon
Airport that brought me back to earth. Then a train to
Dublin and Cookie to meet it.

Getting a job in Dublin is next to impossible for a
foreigner. I didn't find one, so I pared things down and
stayed on the safe side of my uncle's money. Most of the
time, I'm satisfied with dinner in—cooking it and washing
up. There's no VCR or central heating in Cookie's damp
building. He tells me he's lucky to have an electric heater
that works.

Cookie likes to talk, and I listen. The two of us were
eating boiled potatoes and complaining about the missing salt last night when I asked him to level with me. We
both knew I wasn't talking about men or the theater. The
night dragged on, and he talked around the point and got
me lost in his stories.

I know Cookie's repertoire by heart and what vanished
with his brother. The family brains! Cookie is obsessed
with his body—every muscle, every hair. Maybe it's not
compensation; maybe it's the times. These days, there's

not much you can do about the rest of life. Runners take that wisdom for granted. Cookie lifts weights. I watch movies.

I stayed away from back seats in high school and watched my sister and her friends get captured by boys they thought they'd fooled. I was green and willing in college—dismissing the nuns and swallowing the pulp magazines whole. The feminists were after something I thought I had. Freedom.

Tonight Cookie looks worn down, yet his boots are polished and his turtleneck ironed. What is he leading up to?

"Have you read Oscar Wilde? Have you seen the inside of an English prison? An Irish jail?" Cookie is no tour guide.

"I've seen Kilmainham Gaol in a brochure."

"It is for the martyrs," he informs me, pompous as ever.

"One thing I have is an appreciation for terror." I let it go at that.

Jealousy is something I understand, too. I was the tall one with the brains in the sixth grade, but my sister used different words to describe me. It's not easy answering to the name of Skully in Hamtramck. She played dirty and got results. Tripping and pinching, hard. Once, she pulled a handful of hair out of a homemade perm a girl on our block bragged about. Our family's hair is string-straight, to a person. They were fighting in a patch of mud near the ditch, and a crowd gathered. She tried to make the girl swallow a stone. Even boys were afraid of my sister.

So Cookie and I played around with the fate of Oscar Wilde. "He died on the continent." Cookie is so far from illumination, I can't focus him back. I look past Cookie's black eyes, out the window.

I love sleeping with a talker and waking up naked with morning light all over the sheets. The work ethic always seemed like bullshit to me. I cut class in college. Later I found trivial jobs. A few lies and I could stroll into an office before lunch and get sympathy and a sandwich to boot. Sex takes time and space. You can't live in slow motion with an alarm clock and the future on your mind. I never believed there was a future after the sound of Irish poetry left my ears and the summer's stickiness and screams melted into a gray Detroit winter.

Late at night, it's hard not to think of sex: a week of scary initiation. A one-sided summer. Abortion. A flash of romance. Fall. Death. Old-fashioned propositions. Rejections. My own hands in the middle of the night. I avoid cynicism and conclusions and believe, instead, that I have had uncommon bad luck.

Actors talk. They like the sound of their voices. They like a performance and an audience. I figured all that might cheer me up. I expected Cookie to have friends. I expected to meet them. It hasn't worked out that way.

I am a good listener, but what is there to get up for tomorrow? Wasn't Oscar Wilde a dandy? Didn't he carry a cane? I should have a picture of him to get the full benefit of Cookie's ramblings. We sit—Cookie in a dressing gown and me in my flannel pajamas—quoting rhymes from "The Ballad of Reading Gaol." The nuns were big on committing to memory. It's not the only poem I know by heart.

There are some questions I want answered. Where does Cookie get his money? Will this rain ever stop? Am I going to last the year?

8

I am telling Cookie about the heat in Scottsdale and why I left.

Cookie: "We're all scared. Why should the two of you be any different?"

"Have been," I reminded him. "Lucille is dead."

"When I talk to you, I feel like I'm in a court of law!"

We got up late today, and I put the bread in the cooker. We finished off the marmalade and two pots of tea. Then I took out my nail enamel and emery boards, dedicating the morning to my feet. Vanity is a woman's prerogative!

So that's what I did in the way of preparation to meet Noreen, and she introduced me to Father Delaney. I knew a change was coming, but I could never have imagined this one. Noreen is a char who sits in Stephen's Green every Sunday after Mass, and she is proud to be seen with the clergy. Why he sits with her puzzles me. They barely talk.

Noreen covers her hands with white gloves. How long ago was that the fashion in the States? I grew up with sudsy ammonia and cracked floorboards, but we wore rubber gloves and prayed. We are an unlikely pair, Noreen and I, not friends, unlikely to have met, sisters at some point—but not this point. Now it's like throwing stones across a cavern, where we can still hear the sound of loose dirt falling.

The priest is older, balding. His hands are square and freckled. They look soft. He already knows about the Irishman's auto crash. About the contents of my letters that winter. About the whole Reddington family. That Mrs. Reddington became light in the head. What else has Cookie told him?

My boots are muddy, and it's starting to rain again. Noreen has long since left the bench, but the priest and I are holding his umbrella over our heads. Our hands touch.

9

I sleep at the wrong times—either early in the evening or late in the morning. The middle of the night I spent listening to the city and feeling my heart beat—rapidly, much too rapidly. The streetlight at the corner has been out since I arrived. When I stop floating around in James Mason erotica, that priest takes over, the pillow against my stomach . . . his gray eyes . . . I don't know where I am.

Cookie was up and out before I could rub the sleep out of my eyes this morning. As soon as the door closed, I brought out my nail kit again. My mind flashed with images: my feet . . . Lolita's feet . . . Humbert's dingy motel room. Imagine James Mason unshaven, the feel of his five o'clock shadow, the breathless moment when he is lying on the collapsed cot, looking up at the blonde nymphet. It is morning, too.

"Of course I need two shaves a day. All the best people need two shaves a day!"

Lolita whispers: "What will we do now?"

Humbert: "What do you want to do?"

We know what Humbert Humbert wants to do. Mason makes us feel it. And I know what I want to do. My nail enamel is mauve, and I use three coats and a sealer.

Must sex be separate from life?

Where is my life?

Where is sex?

Cookie lives an as-if life. He goes out as if he had a job. He acts as if he were not a homosexual. He behaves as if he loved his dead brother, as if someday he will leave this dreary city. Do his secrets make sense—even in Ireland?

This is a betting country. They love horses. You don't have to see a race to be interested in the outcome. I'll take even money Cookie has moved in with a sure thing. A man who appreciates a bit of gloss. Parasites find what they need. It doesn't have to be you.

10

The weather is getting colder now that the rain has let up. This afternoon Cookie and I ate a smushed apple tart with our fingers and washed it down with tap water. We held off on dinner till late, and finally Cookie told me he's moving out. He didn't say where or why, and he took the ironing board and his picture of Yeats. I'm going to miss both. Yeats looks grand in front of the Abbey. The old Abbey. I almost called Cookie a "rounder" and then thought better of it. He's no ladies' man!

11

I woke up the next morning in a rage because the faucets ran cold. At least, Cookie left his eggcup and teakettle. Along with the splintered furniture—fit for kindling, if worst comes to worst. The eggcup lifted my spirits. A little china thing with a filigreed edge. I took a tray off the shelf, opened the raspberry jam, and was on my way to a proper breakfast, back in bed, when I slid through a pile of underwear, and the whole lot fell out of my hands. The cup in pieces, yolk on the blanket, and a patch of my thigh blistered by the boiling water. I sat down and looked at myself.

When I was fourteen, I had a date with a boy I met at a debate. His parents invited me for dinner and mercifully my father wasn't home when they picked me up. I ran down the steps when I saw their car in the driveway. Their two-story colonial was bare, by comparison, not a knickknack in it.

We were finishing dinner when the boy's mother passed me a china coffee cup, a smaller one than I'd ever seen. I took the cup, not the handle, because that's the way it was handed to me. The burn was so bad, the skin eventually came off the palm of my hand. I'd borrowed my aunt's Sunday dress, and the thought of spilling anything on it scared me. There was more to it. Who ever knows why? I didn't drop the cup or let on what happened. We used Vaseline for everything at home. The jar was big and the label was navy blue. My mother kept it in her top dresser drawer.

It occurred to me, years later, that the woman did it on purpose. The family followed all the other social niceties, and she had served from that demitasse set before. She told me it was a wedding present. Of course she already knew about my father. Everyone did. It's hard to separate what I thought then from what I learned later, but I remember my hand. I got out of washing dishes for a week by bribing my sister. I dried instead and listened to her brag about her boyfriend's new Plymouth.

The point has nothing to do with hot coffee, or manners, or fragile china. But such a lesson, once learned, goes nowhere.

A hopeless situation, here, this morning, too. The sun out for the first time in a fortnight. So I left, with yesterday's clothes on my back and my boots still muddy. I walked to the open market on Moore Street and bought an orange out of a baby carriage.

"Lovely weather," the fat vendor said.

Clichés stay the same, wherever you go.

I admit to some curiosity about Cookie. To dreading Christmas. I stopped for a *Times* and took it to Bewley's where I managed to push through every news story in it. The coffee burned my mouth, and the facts lifted me out of my abortive morning, and soon I felt as good as I ever do, eating my sticky bun and wiping my fingers on my shirt. The high ceilings are some consolation, and a nun spoke to me.

Home again, I shoved the creaky table Cookie left to the back wall and pushed the armchair to the far corner where I sat down and dozed through the afternoon. In my dream, I was eight feet tall and sweat poured from Cookie's face. We were sitting on a high-backed sofa covered with plastic. This time, I picked up one of those individual teapots, the metal ones they used to have in diners, and poured milk in an unending stream into the cup. My hand blistered up like a balloon, and I couldn't let go. Cookie was grinning and I was shaking.

"Hot milk is supposed to put you to sleep," he said. The cup exploded in his hand, and the milk burned through the plastic slipcovers.

12

Dublin is gearing up for the holidays. I took a walk to Brown Thomas and composed a Christmas list in my head on the way. My sister is easy to buy for, and I send her husband a big can of cherry blend every year. Their girls are not so easy, but that is half the fun. I know what the bookstores are bringing out this December and what I'd like to send. But I've given up on their minds. The Irish censors can't hold a candle to my sister. She allows no monsters in her house. She sanitizes Halloween and likes nothing better than a tirade on horror movies. I bought two Aran sweaters instead and thought about those bleak islands and the dead fishermen who wore the sweaters for identification. Then I picked out a porcelain teapot and hoped it would break on the way.

Standing on the bus, with the sack handles digging into my flesh, I had second thoughts about the whole season. Why bother? I always have. Jesus has little to do with it.

I wrapped the gifts in the *Irish Times* and put a flat gold star on each one. The girls will read the paper, and my sister will make fun of my penny-pinching.

I undressed for a proper nap and thought about Cookie and Christmas as I lay there—warm and optimistic—now that the hardest part was packed up and sent to the States. I know what he likes. Leather. Books of photographs. He covets the silver frame at my bedside. Things satisfy him. His face lights up. He talks about his yearnings. He lets you know how he will use the gift before it comes out of the box. He is a child at these times, and I love watching his eyes.

I worked on Father Delaney's present all week, and I finished it after my nap. I narrowed down a map of Dublin, with the streets from his rooms to mine, in red ink. I mashed a silver dove, on its sticky side, right above my signature, *Mary Ben Skully,* with the letters curling around my own version of script. It's the right bird for the season and this country.

13

Christmas was not what I expected. There was a snowstorm Christmas Eve, and the wind had settled down by morning. Cookie went out of town, suddenly, and no package or card came from my sister. I expect almost nothing from her, but I was taken aback when nothing really came. No box to open or complain about.

At noon I opened a jar of preserves, spooned up half, and let the sweetness occupy me. The teakettle stayed on its burner all day, cold. I washed my hair and toweled it dry and dozed off in the chair. The snow did not let up.

At four, I took out a linen cloth and two napkins, a package of white tapers, and a rough iron sunburst. The tapers made a spray of light. When they are lit, you don't notice the holder. I laid out a bottle of brandy and a cake from the bakery and waited.

At nine sharp, Father Delaney came up the steps, his eyes watering from the cold. He shook my hand. His cassock was spotless. He sat down in the armchair. I insisted. I felt free of it, dressed now, warm and sure of talk and the end of his day. Father Delaney has not asked me to call him by his first name, and I never have.

I might have sat in his lap. I wanted to. I had nothing to lose now. But I handed him the map I'd made and cut a piece of cake for each of us.

"How did you get mixed up with the Reddingtons?" I asked. The brandy burned my throat, but I drank more. It isn't easy to confront a man who knows your history. A man of the cloth.

"Merry Christmas, Mary Ben." His voice had a lilt to it.

And then he answered my questions about the family. Mr. Reddington left for parts unknown when they were still children. Mrs. Reddington was a char, so was Father Delaney's mother. It's a hair's difference who was the most ambitious, the most frugal. There the similarity ends. Father Delaney's mother wasn't beautiful; Mrs. Reddington didn't need lipstick or a perm. Cookie was her favorite, but he never thought so. She dressed him in cast-offs from her big houses and bought him candy. Both boys helped her, but Cookie stayed by her side, indoors.

It was pen and ink for his brother. He worked in the States, on the assembly line, long before he met me in the admissions office. Here, he studied, night and day as well. When my Irishman died, Mrs. Reddington could no longer baby Cookie. She knew he wasn't solid, and she couldn't treat him as an ornament anymore. He got a job after school, and she faded away. Lost her nerve. Forgot things. Stopped going to the door. Slept.

Father Delaney helped with the arrangements, and they put her away. Nobody knew where Cookie's money came from then, but he picked up a leather jacket and boots that set him apart, and they were nobody's cast-offs.

Wasn't it a pretty dream—all dressed up with candles and cherubs? The illusion that one mother could feed all those babies! That nothing would stand in the way of their safe journey out? Not even their mother's life. Those right-to-lifers are full of the frightened and the blind. Denial can take you right up to the grave. My sister's husband once fell backwards on the ice, and he was out of his head for five days. My sister laughed: "Charlie always was a joker." I've got nothing against props, but denial never worked for me. Anyway, Protestants made it all into a colorless soup of sorrow and bilge. They took away the joy and loveliness. But it was all lies. What difference do words make in the end? We're alone in a godforsaken universe.

Of course, Father Delaney insists the church is different in Dublin. The church bought him glasses and filled his teeth. He learned math in the fourth grade when he could finally see the blackboard—and the pain in his mouth went away. What does he know? He was as safe behind that cassock as Lucy was in her caftan. She thought her mother was a dispenser of sweets up until the moment she picked up the rock and killed her.

We stiffened up for an argument at the door. He started it: "You're throwing everything out. Why come here to do it? Is the Guinness Brewery any better than General Motors? You're as full of contradictions as any institution."

"Why shouldn't I be? I thought you were the consummate defender of institutions. I'll bet you believe in the army and the asylum. And marriage!"

"I don't believe in the IRA, and I do know the value of a private room." He had his hand on the knob.

"Your room only seems private. Mine has a closet with a suitcase in it half packed." I turned my back before he closed the door.

Months later, I would remember that morning and wonder what Father Delaney thought while it was slipping away. I know everything he said, but what did he think and when did each little part happen—then, or before, in a dream? Did it gush, like molten rock—up and out and on? A burning trap.

It was cold. Christmas was over. It was Monday. Can you think of anything more gloomy? It was no accident. What happened after the accident, that is. I ran in to him on the sidewalk, waving, and affecting a brittle gaiety I didn't feel. The pavement was wet, and I slipped, the second time in a month. I fell on my tailbone, and he helped me back to my rooms. As soon as I was wrapped up in a blanket, in bed, with my sweats still on and my boots in the corner, and he had turned a kitchen chair around—we started to argue.

It was another one of those diatribes where rage poured out so fast, we cut each other off at every turn. I called him a name and started to cry. He got up, sat beside me on the bed, and held me tight enough to draw blood. We had already spent ourselves in words, battles every time we met, perfectly quoted phrases, searing disclosures about our families. This time the words stopped. He kissed me, as soft as his hug had been tight. I wasn't speechless. I said something: "No doubt, you have done this more than once!"

"No doubt, a'tall," he did a fine job of leaving the pressure off my back and putting it in better places. Did I feel happy? Did I feel full? I shut my eyes and listened to the faucet drip, and he started over.

14

After that, I figured Father Delaney would leave me. Alone. A week went by, and cold air passed through the walls. I was brushing my teeth when Cookie knocked.

"What are you taking away this time? The bed?"

"The bed and the chair!" Cookie reeked of whiskey.

"I'm in no mood for a forced bargain hunt."

"I have a proposition for you, Mary Ben." Cookie outlined the details he had been saving up, as he pulled the blanket off the bed. When you're tipsy, the cracks fill in and all seems solid. "What farfetched scheme is this?" I asked.

"Farfetched? You'll be moved within the hour. Do you fancy Merrion Square? There's a grand room for you. With a view of the garden. A desk. All you have to do is be there when I'm not, a weekend, once in a while. A night. Everyone needs a break."

Cookie's benefactor is a rich American from Boston. He is willing to keep Cookie in return for Cookie's promises to keep his house up, to coin a phrase.

I can have free rent to do what I do anyway—stay in! I didn't hesitate.

"My suitcase is packed." I got up and folded sweaters while Cookie finished stripping the bed and stuffed my sheets in the drawstring bag. He left the furniture for the landlady.

"What about a closet?" I stalled at the door.

"A wardrobe? Oh, you'll have that." His boots led the way down and out and on to the bus stop. "And more." Cookie carried my suitcase and bag, and I was left with a purse full of traveler's checks.

15

Who is this American lord of the manor, and when will I meet him? I thought. But I put it to Cookie another way, when we passed each other in the hall of the Merrion Square house. "The desk is grand," I said.

"Stewart Fletcher picked out this furniture himself." He moved on, straightening the pictures nearest the stairs.

"A nice size, too," I said over my shoulder.

"Shall we have a fire tonight?" Cookie seemed pleased with himself.

"Not unless you plan to burn the kitchen chairs." Cookie got my point. He takes care not to spend too much of Mr. Fletcher's money!

Late in the afternoon, after my nap, the turf was delivered, and when Cookie reappeared, around eight, he was greeted by a fire, a bottle of Jameson's, and what appeared to be Waterford crystal to pour it in. Mr. Fletcher's pantry is well stocked.

We sat close to the flames, with our feet on one hassock, and little by little, Mr. Fletcher's itinerary became clear. We have the run of the place until Easter, and Cookie has only to hire a gardener and handyman, in the meantime. "I have a few prospects," he said. "A one-man job for the right man!"

Mr. Fletcher expects summer to come—an idyll with Cookie in a well-managed house—safe from tourists, a jumping-off point, so to speak. Money talks. We listened, Cookie and I, careful not to get in over our heads. Outside thunder rolled and the wind blew hard.

16

Father Delaney borrowed a car from one of Cookie's pals and we drove to the Wicklow mountains. The mountains are high and the air cold. You know those seacoast scenes in the movies. Father Delaney is nothing if not a good listener, and we were determined not to do it again. I told him everything.

That I was just as eager as he was. The widower. It was twice a day, early and late, the whole summer, in his basement. Against the wall. On the mattress. I didn't want less then. I wanted more. And I didn't leave him. His house was up for sale, and it sold, and he left me. My uncle didn't want to believe it, but you could see it. I'm so skinny. The doctor took a risk. A week later it would have been too late. I don't believe in hell or those rabid women who wave banners and picket movies and sway the legislature, but what can I do about my dreams?

Nothing is fair. My sister screwed her brains out in high school. Rubbers finally broke, but they worked for four years. She screwed the coach *and* her algebra teacher. Algebra is abstract. My sister was anchored in the concrete. She laughed at the boys who cried on her pink sweater. I know how they felt. I burned inside and out all those summers, slinging hamburgers at the White Castle. Where is life, anyway? When you're too old and too worn out for it, you find the right moment.

I am quiet for a while, and Father Delaney rubs his leg through his cassock. I said, "That man knew everything but love. We screamed through the walls. Now I live in ice."

Father Delaney took the cap from the whiskey bottle and with thimblelike gestures opened my coat, and then tipped the searing brownness over my lips, kissing me as it ran down my chin. He could have killed me, I was so passive.

"Oh God, oh God," he whispered—inside me, for a moment. I swore. Blasphemous words that carried over the rocks. I felt his hands then, and sunk into it. It didn't take long.

His arms on my shoulders, he felt like a rock himself. My eyes shut. I listened to his shoes crunch the sand till the sounds faded. He returned with a rugby blanket.

I know what he did. He spared himself, tortured himself, and saved me. Saved me what? You can't go against your nature. I pulled his face down into my wool sweater, my hair ratted and dirty, the blanket around us.

"Are you cold?" he said.

The sky was still and gray, and I held on for dear life.

"I can't have babies now," I whispered.

"Oh, Mary Ben, don't you think I know what it's like to give up a dream?"

We lay there. You know how the excitement comes back, sometimes, fast? We were shameless.

We saw each other the next day. "Shall we walk?" he asked.

We walked up and down the quays, never considering a pub, through the park. At the zoo, we watched the animals and children, having some affinity for both. Then we came back to my room and pulled the curtains.

Looking back, I think we had already decided to fasten ourselves to this thing. The afternoon passed and we slept, our heads jammed against the headboard.

Three days later, I told Cookie, "I've hired a gardener for you. Mr. Fletcher will be impressed."

Cookie understands sex and shame and history, and apparently he did not have Father Delaney on a pedestal.

"Where will he sleep?" was all Cookie said.

"There's an attic, if you don't have plans for it."

The attic suits us all. These modern arrangements do not acknowledge guilt. It festers behind the confessional and floats above the couch—unspoken and lethal. You'd never catch me near either one!

We have settled in, the three of us, and labor is divided. Before dawn, Father Delaney gets up and walks out of my room in his robe. I sleep late. He is in the garden or on a ladder, depending on the moisture in the air, when I come down for breakfast. We embrace at the door and drink our tea alone. The stipple plaster takes three coats, and I watch him move the roller, paint oozing, creamy and clean, along the cylinder. It is a timeless life. It feels safe. I scald the glasses and cups in bleach and dry them on paper towels. Cleanliness is next to godliness, isn't it?

17

Stewart Fletcher on the mailbox, Stewart Fletcher's initials on the pale gray stationery in the middle drawer of the library table. Stewart Fletcher's monogram on the soggy bath towels in Cookie's suite. S.F. on the tarnished letter opener on the narrow table in the front hall.

I imagine Stewart Fletcher mucking around in Boston, wishing winter would let up. There's always the water-front and the snowflakes on the Common. *The Verdict* was filmed in Boston, but I am too jumpy to think of James Mason today.

I get up from the kitchen table, deliberately leaving the jam pot uncovered. Crumbs on the floor.

"Who will you get now, Cookie?"

"Why can't you say what you mean, straightaway?"

"Don't think you'll stick me with housework as part of the bargain! I know all about gentlemen's agreements, and I'm no gentleman, and no lady, either!"

Monday morning in walks Noreen, agog at the size of things and Cookie's airs. Before the kettle boils, she is down on her hands and knees. I head for my room and leave the tea to Cookie.

Father Delaney has left the garden and, in full view of Noreen, continues up the stairs, opens my door, and locks it, fast.

There is not much time in anyone's life. Our morning drifts by, my arms above my head, taut. By the time Noreen's mop pail hits the stairs, I wake up with my foot touching the headboard.

Cookie has the jitters at breakfast. We never see him for lunch. He piles his bread with jam and lets it sit when tea rolls around. He spends his evenings reading the papers by the fire. Imagine. The *Times* and the *Boston Globe!* It's Stewart's fortune that pays the bills here, and we are spoiled by convenience and retreat.

At first, I imagined Mr. Fletcher an exotic, but his snap-shots reek of middle age and cover-up. His clothes and poses are not Bostonian. Not a shot on the Common or the Waterfront, no notion of fall or spring—just glimpses at the piano, near the grate, one after another, Mr. Fletcher, alone.

Of course, the camera is not fair.

Stewart Fletcher plays the piano in Boston, and Cookie sings for his supper here, off-key. Dessert is another matter. I fancy I have sampled the dessert and missed the meal!

18

This grand bedroom of mine is long. The desk is long as well, with bowed legs and wood that shines. Along about 2:00 A.M. I wake up. The desk is there, waiting. I take my place behind it. I watch Father Delaney sleep. Sometimes he moves. He doesn't talk in his sleep. He lies on his side, with his feet safely under the covers, and he hugs my pillow. The whole room seems stolen from real life and warm with promise.

At three Cookie comes back. He is alone, on foot. The shower runs, and that's the last noise I hear before I get back in bed. I move my hips where the pillow was. I have made my bed, and I like to lie in it.

Before he leaves each morning, Father Delaney kneels at the foot and watches me. I am waiting for the day when I no longer pretend to be asleep.

19

Outside the wind hammered against the shutters, and I sat by the fire with all the lights burning until midnight. I write letters when I can't sleep, and sometimes I send them. Letters to my sister. Letters to editors. Going back to bed is a relief after they are stamped and sealed—or sometimes thrown away. My pen is filled, and my drawer is stuffed with stationery. Mr. Fletcher isn't the only one who likes to see himself plastered over a blank page. What's the difference between his monogram and my wacky modern letters? A bit of abstraction, that's all!

Today I bought a pencil drawing of Yeats. In it his collar shows his tie and the outline of his sleeve. It's all profile, really. The mouth and eyes soft and wet-looking, and his hair over one brow and a Kewpie curl at the part. He looks young. Pure. Pure, in a way no one can ever be.

20

Father Delaney spent the weekend in the country with his mother. I never ask him about the rest of his life. I don't want to know.

"What class of dinner do you call this?" Cookie sounds like all men.

"Oatmeal and peaches. I was planning a tapioca pudding, but you're out of milk and sugar. Besides, my stomach hurts."

"You didn't have to make dinner." Cookie takes a spoon of oatmeal. "Tinned peaches, slime!"

Cookie takes his time leaving the house, and more time coming back.

I ate slowly and when Cookie returned he heated up some milk and sugar and rattled around the cans in the kitchen. He brought a tray up to my bed and we sat without a word. The floors are bare and lamplight shows up the gloss. I don't remember him leaving.

My dreams pulled me through the twisted bedclothes. In every dream, Cookie's brother was alive again and the ordinary things applied. My navy blue sheets were new, and it was still summer. All I knew about Dublin came from the map in front of *Ulysses* and the Irishman's home-grown stories. Dreams are only make-believe, even if they fill up the night.

I woke up with the flu, and Cookie waited on me—hand and foot.

"Mary Ben, get these bloody papers off the bed so I can make it!"

21

It was an idyll. All winter. But its price skyrocketed with the thaw. How would Cookie justify me, here, without giving away his weekends? His overnights? Father Delaney can answer Cookie's phone now. The garden is more than an ornament—the ivy trimmed, the vegetables planted, the roses in order. More than shutters that no longer bang against the bricks. Blight will spoil his garden and the refuge inside this house if I stay.

I feel some of Lucille's rage, yet I can't bring myself to ruin three lives. Where can Father Delaney find other work in Dublin? Old gossip tearing out his insides, already!

Stewart Fletcher has to see this facade, as smooth as a mirror, and behind the door his monograms. Cookie's flawless profile he has already seen. Cookie's boots moving through the measured hours of a day. Cookie easing Stewart toward safety and exotic sex. Cookie's flat Dublin accent lulling Stewart Fletcher into thinking his performance is not a performance.

22

Cookie has planned a tea party, and I am attending to the details. The house is full of flowers, and the pork butcher knows me by name. I like to have a backup when I entertain: meat pies in the freezer and French brandy in the pantry. It's not my money. Cookie has invited six, but I am ready for a dozen.

Last Sunday Father Delaney and I finally walked through Kilmainham Gaol and spent the rest of the day in bed with trays and newspapers piled up at the foot. It's an exhausting walk there and back, and the history beats you down. Martyrs. And a garrulous old guide to fill in their stories. While we were out, Cookie moved his picture of Yeats over the kitchen table and left the towels in piles of graduated sizes, folded, on the countertop. He also put rainbow mints in cut-glass saucers. Their smell brings back the memory of Lucy's stash. I refused to think about Lucy. I had a bath instead. My legs are weak, and I am as hot as the steamy water I stepped out of.

I want what I wanted all those years when I slept alone in my blue bedroom, growing up—wet, engorged pounding to pull me back into life. I have more reason to want it now. Time is running out—death on my heels and pink, beating love that comes in gulps and waves inside me. I am not sixteen, and I can't wait anymore. I want tonight and tomorrow night. No tea parties or roses or rainstorms. Just Father Delaney behind closed doors.

So we missed the party. Gossip and questions and long answers spread through the downstairs rooms while we pulled our shoulders together in the darkest sleep I have ever known.

How could I leave him?

23

I have the same dream now: running in and out of rooms, past teachers with their grade books dripping red ink. "You don't pass." A baseball diamond with an umpire, all in black, his arm flying, his mouth the size of his head, leaving his face with the letters of his scream already in my eyes—the O choking me. Then to awake and see the tiny blue veins in Father Delaney's eyelids.

The worst part of the dream comes later. Stuttering through French verbs, tied to algebra equations, drowning in formaldehyde. Lying beside a fetus in a big jar, seeing eyes outside the glass. "Your experiment failed!"

What do my dreams have to do with my life? Two degrees gather dust in my closet. I saw through three-by-five cards. Not for me, some prepackaged routine in a linguistic barrel of labels. Let me read what I want. Away from public school English departments in their final stages of decay. Away from publishing houses that sell illiterate prose by football coaches for the "idea" and sure-fire committee rewrite, while a Pulitzer Prize-winner gasses himself in a Louisiana driveway before he sees print.

Dreams drag me through lopsided faces and endless elevator rides where I cannot learn the last theorem or understand the subjunctive.

There are other nights when dreams wait. Nights when Father Delaney and I drink Guinness in bed, exchange uneaten chunks of cheese for the wetness of each other's mouths, nights when it is quiet and dark and his final thrusts become the two of us on a Wicklow hill with the cold air and water pushed away for that brief time when I forget everything but myself and the relief of it.

Father Delaney knows there is no place to live here. We bury ourselves in the quilts and cry and kick the bedpost loose. We have our little fits. We meet the shaky, dry-mouthed dawn, hung over. We walk in the garden together, our legs touching. I can't say what I am thinking. Why do I remember Lucille at times like this? She was sealed away from life. From confusion. From choice. She deserved pity, didn't she?

24

I never knew where my father sat during those Saturday afternoons that began when I was seven. He was a heavy breather—bumping into things. Outside the locked closet, crashes and screams from the radio made it hard for me to hear his customary sounds. I knew the blackness and dust wouldn't last. My mother had to come back from the Saturday matinee eventually.

The hours passed, and I did mean things. I took the clothes off the hangers and wadded them into a pillow and lay down. I rubbed my legs together. With the end of a hanger, I flaked the paint off the baseboards—a little each Saturday. I pulled back the wallpaper in uneven strips. I wanted to pee on the wool coats at the far end of the closet, but I was afraid of the telltale smell. Our closets were small and narrow, and there wasn't room for my hate.

I got so I felt safe in the closet. It took all winter to get to that point. I had a lot of time to think. I didn't want to see my father any more than he wanted to see me. I wanted less, not more. Yet, everywhere I turned, I met a parade of objects. Listen at parties and see how many people talk of getting more. I learned to like off buttons and all-purpose costumes and shoes that had seen better days. Why should I buy a watch when time is hard to avoid?

As the weeks passed, I saw I wouldn't be interrupted. So I curled up with the thought of someone's legs around mine, and my breath gave out.

I think my father hated my questions as much as my face. I'm not pretty and, try as I might, I could not keep my mouth closed. I knew better than to tell, though. We had shut each other out long before the key turned in the lock of that door. I had no allies. I might have told a neighbor. The man next door. If I had been a fool. But I knew even then who I was and how fast I needed to run. My uncle was the one to trust. There are other people like my uncle. He told me that the day he gave me the money. He told me there was nothing wrong with me, and to never forget it.

Most lives proceed numerically from the requisite number of rooms to the requisite number of children. I pay attention to debates over the appropriate year for retirement. I read the obituaries to tally up ordinary results. If you never expand, you never have to pull back, and you can wait in a single room with a closet for the overflow.

25

I dreamed about James Mason last night. We were standing in someone's living room. Other people were there. I had my arm around his waist, and he was wearing a wool sweater. His hair was long, his voice was his voice, still. A bouncer put his hand on my shoulder, and the floor caved in. We landed upright on the basement steps, the three of us. Oriental schoolchildren floated through the high windows, and Mason held out his arms. The bouncer made me leave. When I woke up, it was a comfort to embrace the mattress and wait for the sun to come up.

26

The weather turned warm, and Stewart Fletcher called. His voice held all the proprieties and promised more. Though he and Cookie flooded the house with their talk and plans, Stewart was still just a glossy image until the night I met him in the Shelbourne Hotel lobby and we walked, side by side, to the dining room. The place was quiet, and so were we at first. We started with a pitcher of martinis. The waiter looked surprised and took his time with the order.

"Yes, I like Dublin."

"Yes, I was Cookie's roommate, twice."

"No, I wasn't keen on side trips, but I saw the Wicklow hills once." Were we mired in numbers?

Stewart took charge when the drinks arrived and ordered chateaubriand. We had loosened up some by the time it was served. The soft potatoes and tiny carrots were a relief. Stewart did not have Cookie's tidy habits or European table manners. No buttons missing, but his hair was flyaway, and his jacket needed a press.

"When were you sure?" He knew what I meant.

"I was sent to Deerfield Academy. All those boys! I knew. I had avoided camp and overnights. Three weeks into the semester, and I hardly slept a night. I told the headmaster, and he called my father."

All I know is what Stewart told me then and how sad he looked when he sat across the table. His family is large and their resources larger still. His father teaches history at Boston College. He also gives anonymous scholarships to struggling students in his classes. Four sisters and a house too big for them. A whole wing for Stewart. The yard curved around the block and hid a flower garden. Tulips in the spring and asters in the fall. Fireplaces with delft squares built into the bricks. His parents reading in overstuffed chairs, separated by adjoining doors, like a hotel suite. Maids scrubbing the grates and wood split and dusted without fail. His mother and father were as aloof from objects as they were from each other.

Stewart has never seen their hands touch.

All the children were expected to do was study, and they did—except for his oldest sister who knitted heavy sweaters and tried to watch football games. She was beautiful and slow. His father thought she and Stewart could be fixed, but they drifted out of his reach. Stewart's sister got married, and he ended up at Austin Riggs in Stockbridge. More boys! James Taylor was there, and his brother. Stewart's parents drove up from Boston once a month. His doctor walked with him on the hospital grounds. Eventually snow covered the town.

Money kept Stewart from reality. He had stock in Standard Oil and his mother's head for investments. A Beacon Hill apartment. A summer house on the coast of Maine. Hard rock and rain and time for anything.

Adolescence passed. Stewart left the hospital and moved to Manhattan. Psychiatrists are knee-deep there, and he came with three referrals. He liked them all, but decided on the woman. Soon he was enrolled in Columbia and the owner of a tripod. The snow was no longer fresh, but his rooms had high ceilings and he filled them with New England landscapes.

I interrupted him: "You went to Columbia's film school? I didn't know they had one!"

"School? I came here for the boys. Psychiatry saved me from suicide. Just like being dumb and rich saved my sister. My father hurt more than we ever did. Images and expectations. That's what life is all about. After four years, it seemed to fall in place for me. The doctor and I parted amicably; I was weaned to once a month, then a phone call after dark, her number at the Cape."

"Why so many boys? Is it bathhouse repetition? There are men with devoted lovers. Auden. Ginsberg. Fidelity here and there. Or is it a trance before a mirror? And who is the mirror?"

We were quiet for a few minutes. Does the truth always cut? I like it to. I like it to pass through the gloss and tepid water and clichés and scream out. This may be the only bravery left in the eighties. Risky talk.

"Are the pretty boys marionettes, or are you screwing yourself?"

"I was a pretty boy then."

Stewart was beyond insult. Hiding less than I expected. I can never figure out who likes me. But I was beginning to like him. I ate an olive and leaned closer: "It's hard for me to understand parades, sexual parades. Pectorals. Tans."

Stewart folded his napkin: "Then imagine it's a dream, a raft floating away from safety, not toward it. It costs too much, but the sky seems blue and everyone is young."

The sound of the silverware came through as Stewart served me a second helping of the tender pink meat and watched me eat it. I knew how to tell him what I wanted and not betray Cookie. I understand Cookie, and Stewart Fletcher understands him, too!

"Do you need a receptionist?" I asked, and we laughed so much I had to bite my napkin to regain my composure.

27

We met again for tea the next day at the Shelbourne. Things in my head settled down once Stewart began talking. It was as if we hadn't spent the night apart.

What he'd missed as a child couldn't be recovered—not on a Park Avenue couch or in a Soho loft. Homosexuality has nothing to do with it—and everything, if you see what I mean. Words miss the mark. In those days, he thought photographs didn't. He shot women and children in parks and lobbies and through plate glass windows. He read books on film technique until his eyes burned in a shimmer of 3:00 A.M. madness. By the time he got a degree, he was more alone than ever. Left with a dead world of things and a closet full of cameras.

I realized the magic Stewart was after is only possible in the movies, and then talent has to merge—the writer, the actors, the photographer; and he learned enough to know he is second-rate at all three. If one can never be transformed, one tries to accept things. That bleak snow in Stockbridge is reality, the New England church spire an illusion. New York pretty boys are pretty no longer. They're desperate and dying in the bathrooms of the city with their feet flat out.

Stewart's story ended and the final sentence explained it all: he ended up with a morals charge and nightmares in the daytime.

Stewart Fletcher knows about his limitations, but I can't help hoping there is some magic left in my bedroom in the house on Merrion Square. How much reality can anybody stand?

We are an unlikely crew—the four of us—feeding off each other and the walls. Our hatred of the conventional and Stewart's largesse make our lives possible. Fragile moments of pleasure. Passion and friendship. Holding our pasts in check. Why does it feel like playing house?

28

I have a little more to tell about my family. About Lucy. About the movies. About my mother.

It is not impossible to spend four out of five weekdays fingering the gold earrings and plaid cosmetic cases on Kresge's counters. To dawdle over the reduced summer hats on the way to School Supplies, buy three yellow pencils for a nickel, and wind up the last free hour at the soda fountain sipping a small cherry Coke, consoled by the memory of paying the electric bill, in person, before the heat of the day. My mother did. Detroit Edison had a policy of exchanging, at no charge, used lights bulbs, and this was her excuse for an all-day excursion to accomplish what a postage stamp did for others. True, shopping was only part of it. There were conversations with the handsome Greyhound bus driver, if she were quick enough to arrive while he was counting his change and adjusting the sign from Rochester to Detroit. Later, the druggist, too, took time out for a chat after his delivery boy emerged from the old-fashioned narrow store with the afternoon's emergencies tucked under his arm. My mother had a remarkable sense of timing, so she was accepted in this peripheral way into the working day of others. She had time to spend, if not money.

On my father's paydays she treated herself to a movie and two Milky Ways. Never one to miss the Friday night change of bill, she enjoyed even more the bonus price and air-conditioned darkness of the Wednesday matinee. My father said he was twenty-one and a veteran of two movies before he figured them out. "It's all geared to make me feel I'm the guy up on stage. I'd never fall for a cheat like that." My mother did. And maybe it saved her. It was a life of sorts.

Fed by the trivia and set-up tidbits of gossip in movie magazines, she salvaged a separate existence where the neighborhood, my father, and I caught only her leftover attention. The stars, in color, in full-page pictures looked out of the stack of magazines at her bedside. Maria Montez and Dorothy Lamour vied for first place in fake tropical magazines at her bedside. Joan Crawford stood, hat and padded shoulders aslant, assuring some handsome man that she was right. And middling Betty Grable, with her famous legs and admitted ability to do a little bit of everything but nothing well, posed for cheesecake. And cloying June Allyson's wholesome face was photographed at its best angle. My mother read their life stories, their recent escapades, and followed their nightclub excursions. With a Ritz cracker in one hand, she kicked off her shoes and settled in for what was left of the afternoon before she had to put the potatoes on for supper.

Gary Cooper was her favorite, though she saw her share of musicals and liked cartoons as much as any child. She was partial to that Western hero my father had figured out.

Some of my happiest moments as a child were spent on Friday nights, after the movie, waiting for my mother to lock the garage and open the door to our house. I had the illusion then, standing in the moonlight and smelling the grass my father had cut while we were gone, that I

was an important part of my mother's special times—
nestled in that fantasy mood of happy endings and true
romance that followed us out of the theater as surely as
if it were a third person. My father's insight was a long
time rubbing off on me, and the truth, when it came, was
no consolation. My mother took me along because he
insisted. On his poker night he did not want me sleeping
on the studio couch by the stove: "It don't look good. You
come and go when you damn well please. Take her with
you."

29

I have tried to guess why my mother chose Gary Cooper's
saddle over the melodious voice of James Mason. Cooper
came to town, alone on his horse. He took charge and
saved the day, again and again. Faded plaid shirts and
worn leather belts were her clothes, too. In the movie's
prickly wool seat my mother made the leap to Cooper's
saddle where mastery and salvation seemed as real as its
leather. The question this time: did she land beside him?
Or did she exchange places with him in the darkness of
the movie theater?

James Mason and Gary Cooper? As unlikely a comparison as ever will be made. Best begin with similarities.
There are so few. They both appear tall on the screen.
They are men. They have narrow shoulders. I talk as if
they were still alive.

I did not want to be James Mason. I wanted to be in
the room with the collapsed cot and him to watch over
me in his about-to-be-stolen life. I didn't want to take
charge and save the day, like Cooper. I hate horses and
cardboard Hollywood towns. Good and evil? Like Humbert Humbert, I knew which side I was on and what felt
best. That doesn't make my mother's plight funny. And it
doesn't mean my father learned anything when he figured movies out.

My mother was better off with the darkened theater.

We all got cheated, then. The hard part of deciding what to do now.

All I think about is Lucy. In her cell. In her New York apartment when her mother was in charge of the candy and window shades. Does anyone ever escape? Movies are not escape. People go to the movies to find things, to feel things. Something to embrace. Words. Bodies. Something outside the kitchen. Away from the doghouse. Something clean and whole.

I dream of Lucy in her gallery, alone, with only the lights above the paintings and her thin mints in the narrow box with the crinkly paper. There was nothing clean and whole for her. In my dream, the mints are filled with fluorescent light and the carpet is on fire.

30

I don't pretend to understand my life. I sleep with a priest and work for a man who likes boys. And then there's Cookie. It's impossible to explain. There's then and now. Then I lived in Scottsdale. Now I live in Dublin. Then I had a job and the Irishman and what passed for an ordinary life. Now I have what's left.

Ashtrays

I come from a direct line of women who don't know when to come in out of the rain—much less how. Too headstrong to listen to anyone else or believe what I read in books, I learned the hard way until fate tossed my great-aunt in my lap last summer. I was forty, not long separated, and working for an attorney who wasn't as interested in legalities as he should have been. To top it off, I was still in love with my husband and smoking so much I needed a maid just for the ashtrays.

I've often thought my aunt Claudia was adopted, so different was she from her mother or mine. Claudia stayed home; whereas the rest of the family moved west and tried to conquer themselves. Durham, North Carolina, is not large; and Claudia knows who slept with what tobacco auctioneer and for how long; and she speculates on why they moved on to Raleigh and if they are apt to stay there. The rest of the family cares more about their library cards and bedroom slippers than anything of this world.

I crossed the country and Claudia's front porch, and my life changed, fast. For one thing, my husband and the lawyer and the ashes stayed on the West Coast, while I surrendered to Claudia's rules: "You won't be smokin' them damn things in my house," she said—letting the screen door slam on my suitcase. "And you won't be spendin' your time ruinin' my 'springs either," she continued down the narrow hall to my room, which was directly across from hers. There wasn't much in it: a bed with a light clipped to the headboard, a table, and some shelves. A rocking chair stood by the opened window, and the tobacco factory smell felt like an assault. My suitcase popped open, and my aunt's eyes teared up: "Darlin', ain't

a man alive can resist pussy if it's shoved up in his face."
My husband's picture lay on a mangle of unwashed sun-
dresses. Why hadn't my mother let me in on this secret?
Why hadn't I figured it out on my own?

I stuffed myself with banana pudding, balancing the
dish in my lap, and listened to the train whistle for a
long time before I fell asleep in the rocker. A lightning
bug darted above the vacant lot next to my window.
Would I ever stop missing my husband? We had shared a
pair of pajamas for fifteen years—he in the bottoms and
me yanking the top over my behind. A Barbizon nightgown did not compare.

In the morning, I pulled out a sundress and walked to
the Ninth Street Bakery where I took muffins to go and
skipped the coffee. I was wide awake and ready for cigarettes, and I didn't trust myself. Claudia had had a stroke
a month earlier, and it made cooking impossible. We were
about to run out of desserts made and delivered by her
Bible study class. I didn't want to start this episode of my
life in the kitchen or in a battle with her. My aunt knew a
lot, and I concentrated on that. She knew, for example,
who had gone to Duke and who had gone to hell and the
cost of both trips. She had ridden the elevator to the top
of Duke Chapel and taken a good long look at more than
the countryside. I knew this much from her letters.

That first week I dreamed of ashtrays. Crystal ashtrays
too heavy to lift. China ashtrays, individual ones, that sit
to the right of the fork at those big dinner parties given
by people you never see afterwards. When I could stand
it no longer, I would leave the house and walk. I circled
the East Campus wall with golden girls and dogs that ran
unleashed and stopped on cue—their tongues loose and
dripping. I never thought of getting a job. I had my settle-
ment and my aunt's hospitality. Free room and board,
but it was better than marriage, which offered the same
for a higher price.

The summer stretched before me, hot and dry, and I
continued walking—after lunch while my aunt slept hard
with the phone unplugged; after supper while she filled

up on the game shows. Sometimes I even walked to the laundry—dropping off and moving on. The place was full of those metal ashtrays on pedestals, and even though the room and the ashtrays were empty, the stale smoky memory of what had happened a few hours before drove me wild. The easy part of the week was moving through the color codes of Duke Hospital, making sure my aunt did not have to depend on the kindness of strangers. When I told her about Blanche DuBois and the men in the white coats, she said, "That woman was a fool."

One afternoon in the produce section of Wellspring Grocery, I happened on some peaches that seemed worth the effort. I was taking my time with the sack when a man walked by with an unopened pack of Camels in his hand. Something happened to my resolve, and two minutes later he and I and the sack of peaches were sitting in the sun on the bench outside the store and I was crying. I asked him for a cigarette and smashed it with my shoe a second later.

"Do you like peaches?" I asked.

"Do I like peaches?" He put the Camels in his pocket and we exchanged phone numbers.

It was then I realized my aunt's maxim worked both ways—that I might be able to resist the cigarette or this man, but I couldn't do both. Several weeks passed before I gave in, and then I was more confused than ever—trailing my aunt through the lobby of the Carolina Theatre and listening to her tell about the days when Katharine Hepburn walked across the stage. Such nostalgia distracted me momentarily from any thought of a cigarette.

Imagine the scene inside. Darkness, the popcorn's greasy presence, and me rocking in the newly upholstered seats, ignoring the movie screen, considering the facts of my marriage: a hasty courtship, scraps of affection, faith in the future, and the family tradition of books. My aunt had sold insurance in the heat of thirty Southern summers, and every brick in her house spoke of solidity and plan. Direction. That's what I wanted now, what I hoped to learn from her, but it wasn't a bedtime story she could tell me and I couldn't ask straight up. She had been married too, but that was in the past and she seemed in charge of it—having memorized the photographs, the boredom, and the deathbed scene.

"Do I like peaches?" I thought, in the movie seat, almost pulled in to the English countryside. "Yes, I like the way they drip on your clothes. The sloppiness." My aunt had fallen asleep by this time, and she was snoring softly—her face tan and slack. I finally touched her sleeve, and we left the theater with the others.

In the morning, Claudia brought a cup of Sanka to my bed. "Why don't you try stayin' away from places you connect with smokin'?" She sat down in the rocker, smoothing her skirt and smiling at me.

"The only place I've never smoked is in the shower!"

Next she would recommend needlework! The two of us were not enough for each other. She had the church to fall back on and memories that made sense. What did I have?

That afternoon I enrolled in night school. The class met in a white house inside the wall, as I came to call it, and the teacher talked of opalescence and French civilization. We drank tea and ate madeleines, trying to evoke a remembrance of things past. A summer stroll through Proust? It was more like an uphill climb.

I read each assignment twice, preferring the style and nuance of the novel to my abortive life and no notion of what was coming next. The weeks passed and the nights too. Claudia retired at nine. She hoisted herself out of the tub, passing through a cloud of baby powder, and I could almost feel her collapse after the prayer she soothed herself with, on her knees, her face resting on the chenille spread.

"It's a shame Claudia never got away." My mother's words, as usual, missed the point, but they stayed with me as I burrowed in to the Scott-Moncrieff translation. The book was heavy, and I carried it to the rocker and back, seldom dozing off before midnight.

It had been a mistake to give up cigarettes. I would have been better off sneaking them on the curb in the middle of the night. My dreams exhausted me. In them the sun blazed one minute, and hound dogs cried in neon glare the next—smoke pouring from their nostrils. I woke up at dawn. With a red pen in hand, I searched out Proust's perfect phrases, grateful for Combray and the lime blossoms.

A single thought followed me through the day. What if I sought out men with the passion I have for cigarettes? Would one thing lead to another? Could a morning on a bench propel me underground where roots were bloodred and more dangerous than ashtrays could ever be? Where sorrow, unchanged and perfumed, waited to choke me. And what was the truth? The steady subtraction of power that age brings? Memories that won't go away? Memories of bathhouse betrayal. Of watching a man's life so driven that any shiftless tobacco farmer's seems better by comparison. Theories and therapies and high expectations until the whole of San Francisco was like a running sore, and my husband, frail now and quiet, proclaiming his preference too late. To borrow my aunt's words, my husband is "gay as a daisy," and the truth is I am the fool, not Blanche DuBois.

What else do I have to tell you? Claudia regained the use of her hand—enough, at least, to make cold peach soup, her summer specialty. The man who smokes Camels left town with the American Dance Festival. I am smoking as much as ever and have accepted the risk of an early grave. I still miss my husband, though the effort is pointless, and I can't seem to bring myself to go on to greener pastures. It's not my thick waist and ankles that deter me. There are disguises for those imperfections, and when they are pulled away, the sheets. It's certainly not the diseases. It's just that cigarettes are so accessible. In the worst hours before dawn when my eyes blur and the TV is a buzz, on my aunt's front porch after supper, on every city block, and leaning over the freeway viaducts that move other people out of here: smoke and relief. Show me anything else, in this vale of tears, that works as well. Certainly not peaches or the hands that hold them.

The Polish Girl and the Black Musician

1

"Not here," Ray insisted as his fingers pulled away from Marilyn's pale hand. He remembered stories of how she sucked her husband, a middle-aged musician, all the way from Detroit to St. Louis. Ray knew they came up for air, and cigarettes, and some straight gin from a thermos, but the image made him sweat. The summer of 1950 had been a hot one, too. Now he was back in Michigan with Marilyn, and they were looking for a picnic table in Rouge Park. His car moved onto the two-lane, and Marilyn looked away. The sun beat on the windshield. Ray concentrated on the past. The road seemed to take care of itself. In St. Louis, Marilyn and the musician had lived above a garage.

No air-conditioning. A big mattress on the floor. A bottle of baby oil next to it. Her easels against the wall. She kept perfume and lipstick in the refrigerator, and they sent out for food. Two window fans blew on a Japanese kite nailed to the ceiling.

There was a ragged gardenia bush outside the window. Some of the white flowers had browned, and weeds sprouted up beside the blooms. It didn't matter. Their smell remained.

The musician—his name was Wardell—played alto sax in a group six nights a week, so he liked slow pieces on his night off. Charlie Parker was his favorite. He paced for a while. His white shirt stiff. The same clothes he wore to work. A drink in his hand.

Marilyn wore Bermuda shorts and a faded blouse. She was always barefoot. She leaned against the wall and hugged her knees while she waited to play her Edith Piaf albums. Often a scream from the street stopped what little conversation there was.

I had followed them to St. Louis where I was an intern at the city hospital. I slept in the surgery wing more than I did at home—a rented room eight blocks away. Careful not to wear out my welcome, I measured my visits with the two of them and always arrived with a pint of gin. We drank from the big bottle beside their mattress, so I never saw my offerings after Marilyn took them at the door. It was hard to tell how big her habit was then.

Now she chases her gin with Bitter Lemon. I know the exact nature of her habit. She comes to my room and hugs her legs there. She keeps her blouse buttoned, and I remember exactly how she sucks and spits.

But I'm getting ahead of myself and—keep in mind—we are going backwards. We all lived in Detroit in the beginning. The Rouge Plant still spilled black smoke above the freighters on the Detroit River. Lucky sons of factory workers, with seniority and the UAW on their side, went away to war and returned with two jobs and the GI Bill. The city university was a serious place. There was no football team. Fraternities were a joke.

Before Marilyn met Wardell, she waited in the university snack bar every afternoon with a short professor whose wingtips kept their shine. Every Thursday, she showed up in his philosophy class, a popular one held evenings in the auditorium. She sat in the last seat in the back row. The room was drafty. All winter she wore heavy boots and kept her coat on. She stood alone at break, smoking Pall Malls, as if they meant something. They left together. He walked her to the streetcar and then drove home to St. Clair Shores. He was married.

I saw her again in the French Department, when it was a Victorian monstrosity on Palmer Avenue, speaking Polish to a French instructor from the Alsace. He had a wooden leg. A war injury. With his pointer and the tap-tap-tap of his leg, he terrified first-year students. I thought anything soft had been squished out of him until he noticed her. First he stopped moving. He leaned on the

desk. His pointer was still as he looked at the navy sur-
plus sweater tucked in her gray flannel slacks.

I wish I knew what she told him. She doesn't talk much
now. She never says a word about her dead husband,
though she can go on and on about a book on Monet.
Breathless, her mouth dry, she looks guilty. As if she has
told me too much.

The picnic was my idea. We need to get a few things
straight: insurance policies, the future, my medical practice.

2

Marilyn Niedowitz speaks for herself: Painting is messy,
expensive. My family, especially my mother and aunt, did
not hide their feelings: "What's so pretty about triangles?
A four-year-old can draw circles." My aunt coughed on
her way to the sink to run water on her cigarette. My
father liked me too much. He had a hug that made my
skin crawl.

Alcohol changed my mother's body—bloated it, red-
dened it—but the effect was no different from age itself.
She uses a cane now, and she rarely makes the shift from
pink, fluffy slip-ons to the orthopedic blacks prescribed
by her doctor. Standing with a greasy sack in her hand
outside the neighborhood bakery, a plastic babushka
shielding her permanent, she seems as ordinary as any
Polish grandmother at Mass, but in her kitchen, the glare
of the fluorescent light exposes the acne scars on her
cheeks, her unbleached mustache, and the tremor of her
lip.

We lived in the cleanest house on a clean street. Our
cupboards were stuffed with sudsy ammonia and Olde
English Furniture Polish bought on sale, months ahead,
just in case. Our bleached sheets were so stiff they gave
me bedsores the winter I had whooping cough. White
clapboard with a glossy gray front porch—repainted every
summer—and hosed down every Saturday morning before

the noon whistle blew at the plant. The small patch of grass and snapdragons bordering the sidewalk was weeded and clipped no matter who was sick or working overtime or away at the lake. The medicine chest at our house would have been alphabetized if my mother had had her way. *A* for aspirin, *B* for Bufferin. *D* for Darvon. These distinctions must be made.

A good Polish girl was expected to work in an office at Dodge Main, eventually buy a car, marry a boy with a steady job and family in the neighborhood, and then move out. The niggers were too close. Unlike Southerners, we don't care how high up they get, as long as they don't move next door. In the neighborhood where I grew up, the battleground was clearly defined and the enemy easy to spot—one step beyond Vernor Highway.

College changed everything. A streetcar ride away I met the enemy, and though I will still drink beer, have not dropped the ending on my name, and purposely speak with an accent my aunts and uncles recognize, I have left their lies behind me, near the paint bubbles on their safely white picket fences, resting on the furry petals of their prized African violets. Funky images fill my head now. But mostly, it's Wardell's music. Away. A streetcar ride away.

I learned a lot in the bedrooms off campus, but in the end I preferred my work. All that muck and terror! What of it? And the rooms—there is no comfort in high glossy woodwork and peeling paint. Roaches scatter off the stove tops when the first light hits the grill.

You can spend just so many Sunday mornings nursing a hangover at the S & C Diner. The police are there drinking their free coffee, and temporarily reformed bums in chef's hats toss omelets in the air while something inside you gets eaten away. "A person has got to believe in something, and I believe I'll have another drink." Bad jokes seem too funny.

Sex, that vastly overrated clutching for release, never lives up to its promise. It's messy, all right. That part never bothered me, but Detroit men with brains were victims of tunnel vision and rerun stories of the Depression. And, they all had two jobs. Did I want a quickie? A little something after P.E. and before Chem Lab? No, no thanks. I didn't know if I wanted somebody to hold me or kill me. I asked for the first in a straightforward way, but nighttime walks through three alleys to the art building, with my tools in the pocket of my slicker, made another request.

I wanted long afternoons with sun filtering through window shades, and roses on somebody's wallpaper. I wanted rainy nights reading books with no useful purpose, learning languages spoken anywhere but Poland and Russia. I wanted, most of all, to leave this factory town.

3

Ray continues: After the summer in St. Louis, Wardell was shot at work while trying to break up a fight. I don't know the details, but it spilled out onto the street, and some fool called the police. It was a quiet club. The last place you'd expect trouble: soft lights, thick carpets. The bartender wore a tux.

The Friday of the funeral, I came home with Marilyn. She must have bought a new dress for the occasion. It was long and loose, and she wore some old black sandals with it.

"For God's sake, do something with your hair!"

"Wardell liked it down. Do you think I ever cared what anyone else thought?"

"Where did you get that silver belt?"

"His piano player brought it back from Mexico City."

We sat on the floor, she under the Japanese kite, and me a foot away. Wardell's saxophone lay in its case on the countertop. A row of his white shirts hung in the closet. The gardenia bush was scorched in the September sun.

The room was full of covered dishes and dirty laundry. We sat and smoked until I left for work—stubbing out our cigarettes in a cast-iron roasting pan that still had flecks of meat in the bottom. I couldn't look at her anymore. Instead, my eyes traveled to the tubes of oil paint—the brilliant reds and royal blues oozing from their aluminum boundaries.

I took the bus back to the hospital. At night, all the facts chased each other through my head in a landscape where nothing was anchored down. My glasses and the windowpanes floated through the air, and my hospital bed was covered in blood. The phone interrupted these dreams, and I continued cutting and stitching. Gunshot wounds. A bullet lodged in an earlobe. Throats cut. But nothing was more sudden than Marilyn and her paintbrushes in that hot room, waiting. I had planned and moved and watched and listened. Wanting her. But now the music was gone, and the blinding light of the emergency room leftover.

Getting to know Marilyn and Wardell in Detroit had been no accident. I took a job as a waiter in a black-and-tan on John R because I knew they would be there. Only part-time, my last year of medical school, but it was worth it. The main thing was checking IDs. The club needed business, but they didn't need trouble from the cops.

Wardell had a contract for the summer, and Marilyn waited for him during sets. She got a lot of stares, but nobody messed with her. I thought I was getting somewhere, as I lit her cigarette.

"Do you plan to make a career out of smoking?" I dumped her ashtray and moved my dishrag across the table.

"Why not?" she countered.

I put the hot sauce aside and walked back to the bar.

"You picked the w-r-o-n-g lady," the bartender winked. "Do I need to draw you a picture, son?"

Marilyn's red hair, her silver earrings glittering from the wall of mirrors, behind the bar—they were picture enough.

So I reversed my tactics and got to know Wardell first. When the club closed, the party moved to the West End Hotel, an after-hours spot tucked away off Jefferson.

Wherever they started—Baker's Keyboard Lounge, Trent's, Klein's Show Bar—they all finished up at the West End. I met Miles Davis and Gerry Mulligan there. I met June Christie and her drummer. June Christie didn't like men, and Marilyn didn't like June Christie. The drummer tried to make conversation. Marilyn had grown up with Gene Krupa: "He nodded his way outa high school." That's all she would say. The drummer knew he had reached a dead end.

White tablecloths. Cigar smoke. The elevator going up and down. The police owned a chunk of the place. But you never saw one of them around.

We ate breakfast in Greek Town. It was three blocks from the med school, so I went on from there. Wardell had a laugh that cheered Marilyn right up: "Did you know Mickey Mouse was a rat?" We were stone sober and starving. " 'Course you'll like honey and nuts, and the coffee here will take your head off!" They knew him in those places, and he was a big tipper. You can believe the waiter kept her coffee hot.

The vice squad traveled in black Buicks and wore Hawaiian shirts and stingy brim hats, even in summer. An eight-year-old knew when they were coming. Wardell was as cool as a gust of wind off the river—with them. He kept in light, and you thought it would go on forever. I can still see Marilyn with baklava on her fingers, laughing at everything he said. It was the unexpected stuff that cut the laughter short. They never went to restaurants downtown or on Grand Boulevard. He found a Brillo pad in his scrambled eggs at one, and even Crown Royal couldn't calm him down.

4

Wardell confides in Ray: The trouble with most college girls is they can't shut up. Some have sense and wait with their questions, but sooner or later it's why? who? when? And they all get around to the future too fast. Marilyn was different.

One Christmas morning, she sat in our room at the West End with a bottle of V.O. on the nightstand and her dad's red hunting socks on her feet reading "A Child's Christmas in Wales" out loud. We had checked in after the last set, and the clock was stopped. I'll never forget how I felt—just watchin' her legs and knowin' we had all day. I've had black chicks, Chinese—you know I spent some time in Korea, my first wife was Italian—but they all came at me with this bourgeois shit eventually. And colored women are the worst!

Sometimes I had as much fun propped up beside Marilyn, lookin' out at cars crawlin' by in that gray slush on Beaubien, as layin' her. She gave up a lot for me, and she never said a word about it.

Once we rode a sleeper to New York. Do you remember Birdland? My alimony ate me alive in the fifties. We split a fifth of rotgut and waited for the free champagne. When I saw that blue canopy, the world seemed bent to the right shape.

But her pictures? Too strong. Nobody wants to be hit upside the head with a fuckin' oil painting, and that's exactly her style. Oh, some sold, but a whole helluva lot went to her aunt's attic, and that aunt of hers called her some real bad names.

Things in St. Louis were better, but there was still trouble. In those days the cops thought a mixed couple could mean only one thing. I wore out my wallet pullin' out ID for those bastards. Had to have my marriage license laminated, it got so raggedy. She pretended it didn't bother her.

There ain't much difference, Ray, between cops who bust whores on Brush Street and all those Polacks in Hamtramck. Kill, man. Kill anything dark that won't stay in place. God hates a coward, but they scare the livin' bejesus outa me. I can handle Mr. Charlie till he pins a badge on his suit and carries a gun. Then I'm gone. This nigger ain't waitin' for no sireen!

5

*Ray has the last word: The three-letter word NOW rever-
berated in his brain, and the sound from his nightmares
grew thin in the cold, smoky 5:00 A.M. bed when he woke
to watch Marilyn clutched in a pile of goosedown pillows
with her seersucker nightgown tucked between her legs.
The tiny blue veins in her thighs, her tight asthmatic cough
made him want her more. But having her didn't help now.*

*He saw himself in three years, as scared and still as
she had been this morning—wanting nothing—mashing
out cigarettes in a cracked saucer and eating last night's
fried chicken from a red and white box.*

*Following her from city to city, he had mistaken des-
peration for courage and fallen in love with her silences.
For, as sure as the blood and screams in that St. Louis
lounge, as predictable as her acquiescence, her fat passiv-
ity with men she chose as allies, her beauty, her singular-
ity were more ephemeral than the morning glories that
grew outside her mother's kitchen door. And besides, he
needed a wife, not a mistress. By the time they found
Rouge Park, he had made up his mind.*

*Ray left Marilyn asleep under the red maple they had
leaned against. Dust combined with the sweat on his
beard, drifted past his eyes, and clouded the windshield.
He couldn't afford her—this neighborhood girl who painted
royal blue ovals to fool people. Like a cloudy glass bauble
shaken from a Christmas tree, she lay in the pine straw,
caught in this state where the winters are severe, where it
is customary for "Doe Season" to lure practical deer hunters north for an "easy kill."*

A Jar Cry

When you see a psychiatrist, you learn to wait. First, you wait to stop shaking. Then you wait to start sleeping. Eventually, you begin to see a pattern. Mine is pretty clear. I like older men. "So what?" you say. Well, everything is a matter of degree, and I go too far.

I was tearing up a Kleenex during my appointment Friday afternoon when I really got the doctor rattled. I'm sure there's a reason for that, but I try to keep my mind on my pattern. You learn patterns early, and it takes more than talk and eighty dollars an hour to jolt you loose. The theory is simple: the psychiatrist is a mirror, and your feelings for him reflect the damage your daddy did. So you talk and look hard and wait and maybe, in a year or two, you'll fall in love with a teenager.

The psychiatrist says: "Sometimes brains don't help," but you have to be fairly bright to understand all this. He says: "Patience is a virtue." Not exactly original, but I can't quarrel with the facts. At night, alone in my bed, I stop fighting him and hope I can wait. Passion is hard to resist.

I have an older friend. I see him at family parties during the holidays, and sometimes we have lunch together in town during the off-season. I work for a builder. You know how the housing market is. We don't use names either. He calls me "dear."

Anyway, my friend gave me a lift home, New Year's Eve. Cabs were everywhere and the snow was wet. I was holding his hand in the front seat when I realized it was too late. His hands were soft and strong, like him. I caressed his hand and he mine. Then he put my hand on his leg. It lay there. My head rested on the seat, and I looked straight ahead at the windshield wipers.

"You'd never tell me a lie?" I asked.

"No."

"What will old age be like?" I whispered.

"There will be regrets," he said.

He put his hand on my leg. I covered it with mine. I have always wanted things I couldn't have. Words. Hours. Safety. Like most people, I have spent a lot of time at the window, looking in. The psychiatrist told me there is a difference between desire and action. I want this man in a room with the door shut and the windows open. The air chill. The sheets the same. When I hold his hand, the pleasure of it makes me soft, but no matter how breathless I feel—with his hand on my leg—I know there are words, whispered over and over, I'll never hear. When I remember this night in a pile of sweaty sheets, I will imagine his hands, where mine will be then, moist and deep, holding me—long and close and knowing. Touching me deeper than I have let myself be touched. Perhaps I will scream. I think I remember how to scream. It's done with the mouth open and the back arched, and it comes when you least expect it.

I'm sure I'll have regrets. In fact, I quoted our conversation and my fantasy today, in the hour. I got nowhere.

"You're acting out your feelings for me with this man. He's old enough to be your grandfather. You're damn right there will be regrets. Your conscience will take its pound of flesh, and you'll still be worrying about it when you're thirty!"

You have to tell all, once you begin. That's another rule.

"I told him I was frigid."

"Better an engraved invitation. He's going to fix it, eh? You're not frigid. You pick men with one eye on the clock. He fits right in. He's dying! You won't get a second chance, even at a hundred dollars an hour. Therapy is more than talk. You have to put what you learn into practice."

The doctor drinks a milk shake for lunch. He's tall and thin, and his glasses fall off his nose. "Think of yourself," he says, like a teacher or a best friend. I have to remind myself he went to school for a long time. I have to remember Freud and Marx and somebody else were the three men who laid the intellectual foundation for modern life. I learned that in college—just last year.

"I am thinking of myself—upside down—and swallowing something that doesn't taste like a milk shake." I watch his lips leave the straw.

"You should have gone on stage." He is shocked by nothing. I have given him my repertoire these last two years. I don't smoke, but my nail polish fills up the ashtray, little flakes of it, where I've ruined a ten-dollar manicure.

I live in Hartford, Connecticut—across the street from Mark Twain's house—three blocks from those boring buildings that hold the insurance business from nine to five. I have never wanted a gray life. Mark Twain had a few regrets in his old age. He built that house to see snowflakes through the glass above his fireplace; the architect followed orders faithfully, but after Twain's daughter died, he became a misanthrope. I hate fancy terms. I think he just gave up. My friend who's dying hasn't given up. He has a seductive voice, and he's fond of me. So I plan to hold his hand again and see what happens. I have plenty of problems, so I'm not kissing the psychiatrist good-bye, either. That's a figure of speech. They don't even shake your hand. So many rules. I told him that as I left his office today. I also told him the thought of a teenager makes me retch. They have no regrets. And they have renamed everything and canceled out the future. I think that's worse than falling in love with a dying man.

Synthetics

I sell lingerie at Saks. The hours are perfect, and I like the feel of synthetics. Mornings pass, and a little machine slides the credit cards in and out. Beige. Brown. And no address. Each season has an impression to make and a sale to do away with the leftovers. The mannequins are never bare.

I know all about underwear . . . trendy, but it's a safe life. Gloss. Display. Control. The customers aren't always predictable, but there are boundaries. The longest anybody ever stayed was four hours. A woman trying on bathing suits. That was two years ago before the department split. She continued past lunch. A six with big breasts.

We open at ten o'clock, so it made me wonder if she would be around all day. She left, finally, empty-handed. Careful, though—three at a time, and back on the hangers, without a trace of powder or sweat! The woman who works with me rolled her eyes and took a coffee break. The customer was young. She kept leaning on the mirror and pulling at the straps. She wore a black one-piece for an hour. Demure with a little eyelet on top. She just stood there: "I've had all the help I can stand," she whispered.

You can't bring lingerie back. That's why we hooked up with bathing suits in the first place. Health laws. Now, Resort Wear is downstairs, summer and winter, and we have settled in to the undercover stuff. Bras cover all sizes, and the long-lines are kept behind the counter in a drawer. White only. There are young girls who feel the padding and can't decide on a color. Champagne. Navy. Too many choices. Most people know what they want, and they buy more than one. Some men are in deep trouble. Uplift won't help them, so I try for a big price and keep my voice soft.

Slips are right past the beauty salon, followed by negligees. Now and then we get a woman who needs more than her Friday boost; she is careful with her manicure and very polite. It's the other employees who make you move. The rest room and the sale tables in one breath! There's a rhythm to it.

A week ago, a tall woman came in with a copy of *My Friend Says It's Bulletproof* under her arm and an umbrella with a silver handle. I'm used to money. Those who have it. And those who wish they did. And the ones with no makeup who use their mother's charge. This one took me off guard. I know what that book's about, and—sure enough—she had to be fitted. A double mastectomy.

It's not that she looked bad on the outside. Jackie Onassis is flat. But her voice. Her gestures. Her Chanel suit. Worn but still nubby. Her pearls. It had to be an act, and the perfection of it scared me.

Her hair had little flecks of rain, and even her face was fresh. I couldn't wait on her. She bought everything. A trousseau, so to speak. What wasn't blue was white, and it seemed to float into the boxes. Deliveries are made on Thursdays, and she walked away with her hands free.

I left the floor at noon and took a walk in the rain. It wasn't my lunch hour. "Nothing personal," I said to the woman I work with. "I need to breathe."

This afternoon the customer came back without the umbrella. This time she looked at summer robes and decided on a cotton batiste with blue rosettes. The kind you see in ads. A balcony in Florence with a man in the background and a few words about an Italian airline at the bottom. She was in a hurry, and the elevator sign lit up before I could file her receipt. The second floor here is a circle, so nobody should get lost. I watched her slide past a pram and two face-lifts. The tip of the red arrow, "going down," made me ignore the mirrors on the way there and watch her glide out of my life.

The elevator bell kept ringing, and the usual things pulled me away from the notion I had of following her. What could I have said, anyway? Is batiste soft enough?

Does it ever stop hurting? Can you sleep?

The blacktop outside Saks has softened into a stinking strip between the baked concrete sidewalks. Spike heels are at risk, and the cars in the lot have steering wheels too hot to hold. I feel dizzy before the rotary going down ever begins to twist.

There's a ten-minute lapse before I turn the key in my apartment door and let it crash behind me—rescued by the four walls and silence. In the refrigerator is a bowl of chicken salad, uncovered, waiting. I put it on a tray with a glass of tap water. I can't wait to sit up in bed in my slip and eat the whole thing, fast. By the time I wipe my hands on the sheet and pull out my stationery, the room is cool.

I am in love with the postman. I think about leaving here every day and following his route—hidden by the heat and the traffic. This is my second letter to him. I plan to mail them in the morning.

August 3, 1986

Dear Mr. Fowler:

If you were here, what I'd like most is to dig my fingers into your back and listen to you talk. Maybe you could tell me what old age will be like. How much does independence cost? Is beauty even skin deep? Take your time. I need to relax, more than anything.

Best regards,

Jane Day

I can't pretend now. I don't go to movies. I don't procrastinate. A Pap smear, after fifty, comes twice a year, highly recommended.

Am I entitled to the postman and my two letters? I hope so. I hope he will respond. He lives around the corner in a frame house banked by marigolds. His wife never comes to the door, and the shades are drawn. He could have retired last year, but he kept on. Walking. Giving directions. Dropping off and moving on. It's been an oppressive summer, and I'll bet he'll like my air conditioner!

I change clothes in the evening. Underwear first, then something casual. My breasts sag, but this bra, made in France of imported gray lace, creates an illusion nothing can alter.

I'm sure that tall woman with the batiste nightie would understand my letters better than anyone else. There are some things you must have—this side of the grave. Things that arc not synthetic. Things the postman's wife can't be bothered with.

Four plus Bullshit

There are all kinds of ways to die, and they fall in place if you keep your mind on the categories. Suddenly. Heart attacks. Plane crashes. Then there's suicide. I don't like to think about that. Lingering diseases. The usual way—when the systems wear down, first one, then more, until you're too tired to go on.

My father died in August. Systems. His breath came hard; his stomach ached; his back, too; and one medicine worked for one pain and aggravated the rest. Right back where he started, he waited in a chair and smoked and dozed all summer, the ash falling on the rug.

Finally, he stayed in his pajamas and forgot the books he read. He was partial to Marine heroes and humor. You could never tell what would strike him funny. Once he laughed when his dog bit a meter reader. Our yard was fenced, and that was supposed to make a difference.

In the hospital, the doctor said there was no way out. He would have to stop smoking. Everybody wondered what he would be like without Camels. He had an explosive temper, and all you could do was stay out of his way and wait. At his funeral, one of his buddies from the war said, "Bill was angry every day of his life." I like honesty. It's hard to find after you die. People want to pretty you up—from the undertaker to the mourners. My father called them mealy-mouthed bastards. He had been to a few funerals and he hated bullshit. There is so much of it around these days that his last years must have been hard to live through.

The saddest moment for me came when I saw him watching game shows on TV. He was almost deaf, and he hated television. He didn't buy a set until his second wife wormed her way through his rage, and he never watched it until the last. He was seventy-five. Years ago, he would get up and leave, suddenly, when someone turned on a TV. The novelty had not yet worn off. Sitcom was just a word, not the colorless soup it has come to be. "Who can talk?" he said.

Nothing vicarious for him. Rough and blunt and on the run. He always had two jobs and he stayed outdoors in the summer until the sun went down—weeding, cutting, and pruning. He pruned right to the ground. A little too far. It was good for the shrubbery, but some people couldn't wait that long for the blossoms to come back.

Before the funeral, the undertaker asked me if I knew my grandfather's middle name. "No," I said.

"We need it for the death certificate," he smiled.

"You've got his body on a slab and you need more?"

My father would have put it in other words, but I don't curse in formal settings. My father sold the undertaker the property the funeral home was built on. Funerals are interesting. My stepmother needed a check in advance and a deed to her property before my father could be laid to rest. Collateral. A cash sale. "No exceptions," said the undertaker, his face red.

We moved on to caskets and the soft sell. So many, each less fancy, until the last, which was high-priced. I picked the one with the fresh tree to be planted somewhere in the cemetery. A bonus. My father understood the outdoors, so the extra money didn't matter to me.

"It's a short life," I told the undertaker. He felt at home with clichés and smiled.

At night, growing up, my father was cornered by his dreams. He kicked a hole in the bedroom wall, gradually, and it never woke him up. Snoring, talking in his sleep, he continued on until the sun came up and he lit his first Camel on the living room couch. My mother refused to sleep with him.

Death is like childbirth. People hide the worst. You expect labor pains, but nobody says what going to the toilet will be like afterwards. They all know it but, like so much, you are alone when you find out. Well, my father was out of his head for a day or two before the end. Oxygen. The brain. Systems.

"It's common," the doctor said, after he died. I wasn't there. The doctor told my stepmother he'd be going home in a few days. His head was clear by then.

Death happens fast, and the phone call left me stunned. He got up to go to the bathroom late at night and fell on his IV before he got there. Even that is ordinary. When you die, the sphincter contracts. Who said life is pretty?

Not my father! They clipped his hair and cut his nails and if they could have sewed his finger back on, they would have done that too. A band saw. Nineteen forty-two. Mill-work. Then, as always, the ones with nothing to say complimented his new wife on his appearance. Gray. Everything matched, and he was quiet in the casket.

I went to Saks and bought a black dress. Boots too. High ones. Expensive. It was 100 degrees. I blistered my feet in the airport, coming home, hurrying to the powdery, brittle voices of the uniformed waitresses. The little light above my head clicked off, and I was airborne.

My father paid for my first plane ride. It was a thrill. I took notes on the clouds and the passengers and drank too much free champagne. New York has never looked better. After a rainstorm, at midnight. I was twenty-one.

My father once told me he'd like to die behind a lawn mower on a sunny day. The sweat, the grass, the click-click. He used a push mower. He loved the Chinese elm in his backyard, and I can see him under it, with bulging muscles and tattooed arms—talking about the Boxer Rebellion. He was shipped to China, a Marine, sixteen years old, to protect American oil interests. He had run away from military school and lied about his age. Incorrigible.

Death is hard to avoid. I'm fifty, and it's waiting in the wings. I don't smoke Camels or have any fantasies about lawn mowers. But I'm scared too. And when I think of my father, I feel lonesome for all he gave me and all he couldn't. Most of all, I miss his voice: "What the hell is four plus bullshit?" he would have said.

"Just a medical term. You can't miss it under a microscope. Like a positive Wassermann!" He would have laughed, choking on the smoke from his cigarette.

Every House Connected

Ginkgo trees have heavy leaves, and they fall in piles that never rustle—yellowed, subdued, barely dead. Georgetown sidewalks are made of brick and the ginkgo leaves soften each crack. Townhouses. Every house connected. Every garden walled. How could boundaries not matter on a street like this?

I stay indoors in the afternoon, and my favorite place is the tub on the third floor. The skylight is covered with pinestraw. A random seed—not part of any pattern. The steam feels good, and my dreams roll into the light on my bedside table.

This morning, after my run, I stopped to watch a bride and her flower girl in front of the Capitol City Club. My head pounded and my face was cold. Neither the canopy nor the heavy velvet—she wore cream, the child burgundy—offered much protection from the rain. Fifty-five degrees and falling. It is November, and I am married too.

Twenty-six years. To the same man. A love match. My dress was white and the nights flew by in a wet, hot haze. I miss the tenderness. My husband changed and the girls scattered themselves from Seattle to Mexico City. One even got to Japan—pushing the ocean aside as if it were nothing.

"The ginkgo trees are bare here," my daughter writes from Kyoto. Black ink seeps through the rice paper on my leg.

What happened to me? I ran everywhere and lost track. The Capitol. The Library of Congress. The big hotels. The bridges. My eyes averted from the other runners who passed me—single-minded—trying to remember the way back.

A different sort of steam hovered above the grates on Wisconsin Avenue. A man, with a loaf of Wonder Bread at his feet, cracked his knuckles and looked at my legs. Homeless. Without letters, or voices on the phone, or house dust—he sits—his umbrella failed, his gloves torn.

My legs disturb him.

Lunch is the same price as dinner in the restaurants along M Street, so I don't stop. The Biograph organizes the movies by country and calls it a festival! There is no matinee. The homeless man won't be going inside for lunch or dinner, and he is spared the smart talk in the lobby and the movie. He is wide and black and has what I think is an Indian nose. I'm mixed too. Irish enough to know nine-year-olds murder each other in the alleys of Belfast, and Poles, like my father, are buried with the Jews in Warsaw. Death is more real than my Catholicism.

I'd like to give myself away this year. Surrender. I suppose that's what appealed to me about running. I thought it would clear my head if I gave in to its forms. The shoes, the carbohydrates, the jargon, the air. Like a bone buried in the desert, I felt the day would emerge—hard and white and clean.

After forty-nine, the body is best left covered. Towels. Underwear. It doesn't matter. My bed is strewn with letters, and it's hard to pull out my pajamas. In dreams I know what to expect, and my heart feels like a sapphire—cold and blue and solid.

Most weekends, I stop in a bookstore on Dupont Circle. The clerk tells his girl about who he won't let stay, and she looks at the book bindings. She has a hole in the arm of her sweater, sturdy legs, and, if you can seem excited and exhausted at the same time, she does. All day the clerk decides who will take home money. Some books are worthless. The rocker is unsteady. I sit, overlooked, lost in movie memorabilia. James Mason as an Irish rebel and finally an English baron offering up the Lord's Prayer to his dying gamekeeper. My head buzzes with Mason's words. Why is it my own husband's Last Rites left me dry-eyed and steady? My husband had a brogue that could carry me off to sleep and a back that remained straight and, once, when we drank all the whiskey we could hold, he sang three verses of "Molly Malone" on a Charleston golf course. To me. We were naked, and it was three in the morning.

I fell asleep last night with my vibrator plugged in. A nasty sore. Deep. In the side of my leg. A part where the flesh is softest. I'd had too much to drink. It would never have happened on an ordinary night, because I can't sleep, even after the release. I always put it back in the drawer and wait, listening to gangs of college students walk by, laughing, offering themselves up to the darkness.

I took my last exam in 1961: Contemporary British Writers—A Survey. "You're born, you live, and you die" was as much philosophy as Arnold Bennett could come up with. And James Joyce, being Irish, was not included. I got out of bed and played "On the Road to Mandalay" on the piano. Martial music, even in the nation's capitol, is hard to find at that hour. The window was open, and someone bumped into the trash cans. I sat in my love seat and watched the wind blow the sheet music on the floor.

This morning the ginkgo trees look like sentinels, and the garbage trucks have come and gone. A squirrel sleeps on a dented lid. It is only when I reach level ground that I realize I have never seen a sleeping squirrel, and this one is not sleeping either. I turn back. I can't get in the tub fast enough and I stay there a long time. The rain doesn't stop its splash against the skylight.

I shouldn't complain. It rains night and day on the West Coast. My daughter in Seattle made friends with a middle-aged writer who bypasses the days and nights and the rain. She types with the shades drawn and drinks a martini the first ten minutes of *The Today Show*. Then she sleeps through. The writer is a lesbian, according to my oldest, the one with the grant, who examines Japanese ceremonies and literary suicides. What does that have to do with anything? The bedroom should be private, and scholarship should make sense. What connection can anyone find between pouring tea and tearing out your insides with a ten-inch blade? Frankly, right-wingers terrify me, even if they're Japanese and have style.

My daughters are drawn to fragments. Bleak, cracked color in a frame is art, but any novel over ninety-five pages is too discursive to qualify! The music they listen to makes me twitch in a chair. Dissonant. The overture missing. More burden than relief.

Consider maternity. This year I have time to think about it. Close, but never close, my girls were born in the fall, as regular as any harvest, until I realized what is natural and advised is deadly, too. They almost had two sisters. The days and nights did not end but congealed around sand and snowsuits and cough syrup and a million crushed cans of Minute Maid. I changed doctors and hospitals and rhythms—saving my life and breaking the rules with a tiny coil the new doctor said would help me relax. My husband wanted a son.

"You have betrayed me," he said, in the flat voice he used with his secretary. Fallen away from the candles and beads and merciful darkness, I believed him.

And what was sex then? Silent and quick and gray—the mystery gone. My nipples sore from the futility of it.

After that, I did my kneeling on the kitchen floor and became a slave to order.

"I grew up starched and ironed and there's no way I can be wrinkled!" I forget which daughter said it first. They stood outside in their navy and gray jumpers—displaying a united front to the nuns and relatives while they burrowed underground to what mattered—bypassing my polished surfaces and their father's diminished expectations.

Softer words bind us now: stories, gossip, secrets. Fragments woven through a woman's life, for even my youngest in Mexico is a woman at long last. "Isobel," she tells me, "you live in the middle of everything!" I read her letters as I once read her poems—searching for that perfect phrase that holds life for a moment and sears the air with its clarity: for, after all, it is your children who remain when other dalliances are past and winter comes in a rush. It is some solace to know she, the one I didn't want, is the one pulled by the sun. And every revolution. As for me, passion is out of the question.

Other People Shudder

I wasn't ready for summer, and now it's over. A child psychiatrist is teaching my daughter to play solitaire, and I'm not sure what's coming next. At night the dry grass in the half-moon's light belongs to no special season, and all along the highway the kudzu is dying.

I try to content myself with notes to the milkman and daily stops at the Farmer's Market. Here in Georgia people pay attention to vegetables, and the market is far enough away to fill the morning. While supper simmers in the crock, I look out the window and wait for the mail. Too often there is postage due.

We see the psychiatrist on Tuesday afternoons before school lets out. Yellow minibuses are lined up on the baked concrete waiting for the others. It's a three-mile drive past a body shop and two car dealerships. We park near the door, enclosed between the lines for compact cars, and we hurry up the steps of a redone Victorian house with a brass knocker nobody uses. I bring insurance forms and flash cards, but I can't help looking at the others.

It's a big waiting room with window seats. Some patients bring their whole family. Parents. Brothers. Sometimes a grandmother. They either say nothing or talk a lot. One cross-eyed boy makes a stack of *People* magazines that keeps falling over. He looks surprised every time. The psychiatrist is a Cuban exile; she makes a specialty out of treating mothers of handicapped children. There are muddy wheelchair tracks on the carpet on days when it rains. One patient, who hears voices, rides his bicycle right into her office, careful not to let the handlebars touch the wallpaper, and telling his voice to "pipe down."

Before the revolution, a manicurist came to the house every Friday. The aunts and nieces gathered in the psychiatrist's bedroom and drank Cokes. Lemon trees grew in the courtyard. Music played. Imagine the ease! She also told me she treated a girl like my daughter who learned to wash chemistry beakers in a college lab and run in the Special Olympics.

"A protected environment," her Spanish accent trails off, and the psychiatrist bites her nails. The Special Olympics was a TV extravaganza this summer. The Kennedys were there, perhaps remembering the days when Rose thought her daughter could be repaired and protected.

Last fall my daughter's only friend got a job at Morrison's Cafeteria, but the manager liked her too much and when she told what he did to her in the parking lot between football season and the Super Bowl, he was fired and she went to a group home.

Today my daughter walked right in, and I was left with my thoughts. A man on the other end of the couch was waiting too. Looking around and seeing only me, he lit up and put the ash in his Coke can—caffeine-free and still icy around the edges. The smoke made me laugh. Do you know any doctor's office without those death threats or thank-yous in red ink plastered on the wall?

Until recently, I was devious too. Now I explode at parties before the pastry tray arrives and go berserk at the Honda dealer's. Late in the day, those lines and extra charges and all the phony promises are too much to bear.

Last year I read some Cuban history and was surprised to find Castro is an attorney. His camouflage jackets and big cigars fooled me. I was drawn into his imagery. Seeming for a while to be master of his fate. Like all of us, he's older now and world events have reduced his sunny island to its original size. Our fears have shifted to other places.

The psychiatrist's voice helps as much as her words. I think of it at night when I try to sleep. I think of Cuba and Batista and the dead—and the clean hope the revolutionaries started out with—and then I consider politics. A second boatload of Cuban criminals and defectives arrived in Atlanta a while back. They were caged and discussed. Castro's sly. The psychiatrist talks fast when his name is mentioned. It's not protocol to concentrate on personal horror if it's not the patient's, but I'm sure someone she loved hard was left behind to die. A sister? An aunt? Maybe the manicurist was more than a manicurist.

I believe in the Statue of Liberty and people yearning to be free, even though it doesn't make sense anymore. I'm not sure what sense is.

The Catholics consider my daughter a gift. I have a Catholic friend, and the psychiatrist is Catholic. She was brought up with all that beauty and ritual. Flowers, robes, and, above the hard earth, the cool altar. Solace then. Before the revolution.

The man on the other end of the couch has finished his cigarette.

"When is it going to rain?" he asks.

The man looks at my ankles. They are bare. I stopped shaving my legs five years ago. It was hard enough to get up in the morning.

"Last summer was worse," I say.

"It's cooler in the mountains." He shoves forward.

"I have a big air conditioner." This stops him.

It makes no sense to flirt here. Whoever said empathy leads to romance never suffered. I need a man without this kind of anguish, so he has room for me and my daughter. My husband left us on the Fourth of July before the fireworks. He chose a blonde with designer glasses and an inheritance who considers *Gone with the Wind* a masterpiece. She is partial to men with tight hindquarters and words like "supportive." I try to drift out of their sphere when I'm awake. I try to forget she runs a special-ed camp across the Chattahoochee River, and I'm the one whose gratitude knew no boundaries.

"Let's invite her to lunch," I said—with nothing on my mind but the menu. She was so cheerful I mistook it for joy. In the beginning.

"I love your daughter," she said, lowering her eyes in a sincere pose.

"A good mechanic," I overheard my husband tell his brother.

I wish them well.

"Your husband has an escape fantasy," the exiled psychiatrist says, with a prescription in her hand and my daughter at her side. A tall child with French braids and eyes askew. She holds a deck of cards in her hands and grins.

Solitaire is a strategy. There is no escape. I remain mired in the ordinary, and I know chemistry beakers shatter and no environment is protected.

Going home, rain clouds slide through the sky, and Paul Simon reminds me even "Charley, the fat archangel, files for divorce." I have a sunroof, and my daughter loves it and me. That's enough when you think of the alternatives.

Emmett Till and the Men Who Killed Him

I never really knew my uncle. He lived somewhere apart from the places he went and the things he touched. Eventually I saw some of those places and a few of those things. I even learned some facts about his life before I was born, but in the beginning, he was twenty dollars at Christmas and a laugh that scared me every Saturday morning. There wasn't room for me and my uncle in the house I grew up in.

It was a one-bedroom frame built on a slab and paid for as it went up. At first, there were no walls separating us, then came drywall, plaster, and finally paint and baseboards. I slept on the studio couch next to the oil stove, and my uncle had the davenport across the room on his weekend visits. He snored and slept in his undershirt.

On Saturday afternoons in the summer my father's friends drank beer in the backyard and traded stories. The cut grass was damp, and flecks of it stuck to their shoes. My mother made lemonade in a pitcher she won at the movies. It was wartime, and sugar and gas were hoarded. Not by us. By the Jews. My father knew what was going on outside our fenced yard.

"The niggers are taking over the factories," he said.

The Japs were, however, far away. I saw them nose-dive in tiny planes at crowded movie theaters where my mother was one of the faithful—a fat woman in a print housedress and warped brown shoes.

"You have nice feet," she said, and she bought me Buster Browns because her mother had forced her feet into shoes she had already outgrown. My mother took me to the dentist for the same reason. She hated the sight of her crooked teeth in the mirror. When the bills came, my father said, "You find out who your friends are when you need money."

I tried to put their maxims and sacrifices together to make something to live by, but there were too many missing parts—told in whispers and not to me.

My uncle seemed like a man of the world. He lived in the city. Twenty miles from our subdivision. A bachelor who chain-smoked in his rented room piled high with newspapers. One or two tall beer bottles lay on the floor next to his gray work pants. The air was undeniably his.

We picked him up outside the National Biscuit Company when the night shift changed on Friday and drove to a steak house where we ordered for three and asked for an extra plate. He paid for it. I was glad to be included, and I kept my mouth shut. My father did most of the talking. He told stories I didn't understand about the past—in Arkansas, Louisiana, and southern Illinois. We took the early edition of the *Detroit News* home with us, and sometimes my father carried me on his shoulders.

My uncle had a college degree. He was the first grown-up I knew who had finished high school, but all he read was the paper and Mickey Spillane. In 1930, liberal arts at Centenary College included French and world history and physics. My uncle made As in all of them. I saw for myself a cardboard box with his school records and a snapshot of his family the year before his parents and four sisters died. The flu epidemic of 1918. My uncle was twelve. My father was a baby.

My father said my uncle had been jilted. My mother said: "He makes me nervous." After their fights, they insisted I call my uncle "Sir."

When I was twelve, I saw two movies that made me think I understood more than I did. *Gentleman's Agreement* and *Home of the Brave*. Message movies, they were called. All about injustice and victims and pain and being left out. The villains in those movies couldn't hold a candle to my uncle. He said: "Niggers should be shot." The set of his mouth and the look in his eyes made me feel he might shoot one. My father was a hunter, and guns were everywhere.

"Give 'em an inch, and they'll take a mile!" My mother

told me a hundred times there was one colored boy in her high school, and everybody l-o-v-e-d him.

My father said, "I took up boxing till they put a nigger in the ring. Then I quit. Their heads are harder."

At the National Biscuit Company, my uncle was a foreman. He checked the saltines for thirty years to make sure they were neither burned nor doughy.

"Niggers are everywhere," he told me.

I saw them once. The room was hot, and my uncle wore a white apron. It was a private tour. The niggers laughed —their white collars limp, looking at the flour on their shoes. My uncle's neck stiffened, and he dropped a tray of Ritz crackers on me.

I decided then my father's guns were safe. My uncle was alone. Unmatched in his hate. He seemed to be laughing at me and my parents, who had been fooled by desire and marriage and the scraps of pleasure we rubbed up against, that he paid for. Finally, Republic Aircraft shut down, after the Japs had been subdued. We had sugar for our lemonade. The Jews bought up the scrap metal, and my father was out of work.

"A livink, ve got to mik it!" My father did his best to imitate a Yiddish accent. He was the only one who ever thought it was funny.

I imagined I understood them all by the time I entered college and made my own *As* in psychology and American history. Certainly, when I fell in love and was left flat by the urbane man who was miles away from our meager Christmases and muddy subdivision. Scholarships. Fellowships. Summer jobs. Independence.

The National Biscuit Company closed its Detroit plant, and my uncle moved back to Arkansas and became a recluse. The newspapers blew the sixties through our brains, and I made my voice known in the picket lines outside Woolworth's and read about Viola Liuzzo's journey south. My father crossed a picket line too, and goons from the Teamster's gave him a six-inch scar and a story to tell for the rest of his life. Unemployment. Hard rock. Fire. The 101st Airborne came to town to quell the riots, and a cop told my husband in the emergency room at Receiving Hospital: "I'm goin' out to shoot another nigger." The Algiers Motel was not an "incident." Boundaries were gone, and anything was happening.

Emmett Till left Chicago to visit relatives in Mississippi. He whistled at a white woman standing on the hot sidewalk and before the sun went down he was buried in concrete.

I knew my uncle could have done it if he had been in Mississippi with the mob. He could have done worse if he had been in the right place with the others. He was outnumbered at National Biscuit. Instead, he played solitaire and grew old and died on six acres of scrub pine. After the sixties died down.

What happened to him?

I don't think losing his mother or being jilted explains it. Or raising my father. Or money. He had a scholarship too. Neither the Depression, the war, nor the South gets at the horror. Who ever knows why? But I have long since stopped feeling superior to him. I, after all, took his money, and that is nothing to be proud of.

I travel in circles where his words are never spoken, and bitterness is disguised as wisdom. So much is private in life! Like the moment when Emmett Till realized his whistle was a death rattle, and the moment those men went home and ate their suppers in the heat with wet concrete on their pants, bragging, in my uncle's voice.

Hildegarde's Long White Gloves

"**L**ife is not a fashion statement," I told my friend Paula in front of a vintage clothing store in Chapel Hill. Paula opened the door and walked through capes and jewelry before she reached a row of crepe dresses smashed so close it was an aerobic exercise to look at each one.

"Move down! It's all mixed up, and you have to keep on going to get anywhere." This to a black man with a razored brush cut, adjusting his Carolina blue T-shirt. He didn't budge.

The only place navy crepe looks right is Sunday School, and Mary dropped that like a flatiron the day she got married. Methodists hanker after order and restraint: 10 percent tithes, the chipped cup on the back shelf, weak tea at wedding receptions. John Wesley was austere. An Englishman. There's no doubt Paula married beneath herself—a foot-washin' Baptist with dark eyes. He ignored a few rules, and at least she could breathe.

Six people stood in line for a makeshift dressing room behind a curtain. The black man told Paula to be patient. I recognized the accent—South African—an education built on gold. The King's English. Shoes from Johnston & Murphy.

It's your funeral, I thought.

Saturdays are like this in a college town. Too full.

"Why buy a dress with buttons guaranteed to fly off the first time you pull it over your head? A garment some wife 'made do' while her husband was getting his feet wet in the Normandy invasion. What's so great about the past? Bag it. I don't like art deco or thrift shops or the smells in a closet after someone dies. Antiques are rickety and no bargain either. I'm worn down too, but nobody is searching me out at reduced rates."

"You've got a future," Paula told me at the cash register. She never tries anything on. And she can't predict my future or hers.

"Two dollars and forty cents—no tax on clothes." The clerk has spiked hair in three separate shades.

"She's a statement too." I keep this to myself and rip off a hangnail. From there we go next door to Modern Times and look up. Knit dresses on one wall and jewelry on another. Silver ballet shoes on the floor, and behind the scenes fabric in piles against the fingers of three women in front of three sewing machines. There's a chair to sit in. I sit. Paula tries the patience of the owner—a tall blonde with a diamond in her nose and more sense than Paula will ever have. She shows Paula all the colors and wraps them around her defects. Paula buys a head-wrap, and we leave.

"The look is too strong, Paula." Sometimes my eyes scare me. "I suppose you're going to wear them together."

"Huh?"

"The head-wrap with the dress, Paula."

It's a shame to waste this October light that hangs around for a few days and then gives in to rain. My mother taught me to rise above my surroundings, so I focus on the weather. The leaves are noisy. We pass McDonald's and Pyewacket. Their parking lots are full, and the smells from each place mixed up. Somebody told me fast-food joints put poison in the burgers to keep street people from getting fat. I don't believe everything I hear. Paula can't stand the light in either place. I am starting to get a blister on my heel.

It's a short mile to the Carolina Coffee House, and Paula clips it off, uphill, with the Modern Times sack under her arm, her purse handle loose and flying. She needs a haircut, but she can't think that far ahead. How would one of those asymmetrical sideshows look on a fat woman with her slip showing?

"This place reminds me of Vienna," Paula says as we push our way onto the cushions and light up. The booths are dark and tall, and candles are already burning. The tobacco factories in Durham may be down to one, but who cares? I have a friend in Toronto who sends me Cuban cigars that cost $2.75 each. We were lovers in 1971.

"A martini—arid," Paula tells the waiter.

"Arid?" I say.

"Don't you know anything?" The waiter looks up from the bar. The crystal and ice—the bottle. All before my silence penetrates Paula.

"Stolichnaya. Stoli. *The* vodka. Wake up."

I make sure my napkin is in place and the salt is close by.

"Nothing. I know nothing!" I let that settle in and decide on a double plate of asparagus and some water. "When did you go to Vienna?" She's never been farther than San Antonio, and she hates snow.

"This place seems like Vienna," she revises herself, dillydallying with the vinegar bottle.

Paula likes Vivaldi and the antique lamp on the bar. I've been here before and I know what's coming—Bach and chocolate pie and real cream for the coffee. I need it all because Paula doesn't know when to quit.

"Try the soup." She ignores me.

"Nobody can spoil a baked potato."

"I couldn't abide my mother's rice pudding. Why should I swallow your vegetarian bullshit? Homemade, huh?"

In a few minutes Paula will start: "You're a fool . . . stuck in the house . . . stuck with a job . . . wearing that half-assed preppie uniform!"

I've known Paula thirty-five years. Our mothers were neighbors. I grew up in their kitchen, and the only antique Paula had then was a wood-burning stove. Big and black with grease caked on the wall behind it. When I was eleven and Paula thirteen, my mother bought a Philco radio and we listened to it all day. I had a crush on Hildegarde. Unburdened by a last name or Southern accent, she breathed out, "Darling, je veux same beaucoup, je ne sais pas what to do. Darling, you've completely stolen my heart."

Blonde. Small. Hildegarde wore white gloves and sang in a voice that made me shiver. Were those gloves long? Did they have pearls at the wrist? So many wars since then. Things get confused, and my memory is bad.

"Please take me to see Hildegarde." I dried each dish and broke the colored capsule in the oleo while my mother hummed her own tune and considered her Jello collection.

I had stolen a pair of white angora gloves from the Christmas sale table at Sears, and a 300-pound store detective stopped me outside the double doors. Wordless, I followed her mincing steps to a room in the back and, as she sat on a bench and listed the consequences of my greed on her fingers, I looked at the floor. The room smelled like cabbage. I had a piece of stale Juicy Fruit in my mouth, and I tried hard for the leftover sweetness. "Don't you know gluttony is a sin too?" she said, tilting my chin with her swollen fingers so that I had to see the whole of her and myself. I have never been able to do that again. Evil is impossible to confront, and anybody who tells you therapy makes you feel good is a bald-faced liar.

I went to school with her niece: ". . . nice girl . . . Annie picks peaches in the summer and helps her mother . . . she even has a job at the five and dime. . . ." Her praise left no room for the real niece. Like a crazed preacher lost in his own sin, she talked louder and longer and less to me than to an unconvinced part of herself.

I never forgot that girl's name: Ann Bates. The Ann Bates I stayed away from knew all about trade-offs. She read geography over the shoulder of the cripple and then made him swallow a marble when recess blew the chalk dust and monotony away. She entertained the varsity in the back of her brother's pickup and became a cheerleader without one split to her credit. And this breathless aunt of Ann Bates's had a job and benefits at Sears, while my mother took in laundry and crocheted lace pot holders nobody wanted, in six pastel colors. When my mother arrived and promised the heaving boatlike woman something in a whisper, my mother turned, red-faced, and shoved me ahead: "You can have anything you want, just ask me." We walked the length of the store, side by side.

"Anything I want?" I knew she couldn't mean things. My father made eighty dollars a week. He had lost two fingers to a band saw and reminded us how insubstantial the world really was every time he worked the Lava soap over his palms.

I figured she must mean what I really wanted. Something good that wouldn't wear out. A memory. A moment. The Philco had come on time from People's Outfitting Company. Voices are not a whole memory. "La Vie en Rose" wasn't enough. I had to see Hildegarde's long white gloves.

Summer passed. Hildegarde was coming to sing in the Capitol, in a hotel. I washed the dishes and dried the cups while my mother took the clothes off the line. I could walk back, I thought to myself as the last jelly glass touched the oilcloth. I saw myself smack in the middle of the two-lane, the gravel on fire. Weak with pleasure, I waited to rake the dirt in the front yard.

August. Dog days. School about to start.

"I don't need shoes," I screamed as my mother dampened the cottons and rolled them in perfect cylinders, a Camel wet in the corner of her mouth. She looked down at me.

"Please take me to see Hildegarde," I whispered.

"You're a little girl," my mother laughed. She pulled a plate of fried potatoes from the icebox and ate them, standing at the kitchen sink. I looked down at my feet and never mentioned Hildegarde again.

The rest of August, after every meal, I bounced a rubber ball off the utility room wall and caught it. My mother stayed inside and let the dishes drain in the sink. She kept the radio low.

The war ended at five o'clock on a Tuesday and a string of kids marched by our porch with pots and spoons banging out a message I never understood. I threw the ball in the ditch where mud covered it. Paula understood why I left it there. She hates mud and rainstorms and lies as much as I do.

The waiter is avoiding us, and Paula's voice is loud: "Don't swallow that crap about romance under a tin roof and the sound of rain being cozy. It's right up there with Bible School and virginity and class reunions. Right up against 'Just let me put the tip in.' "

Paula eats an olive and looks at the waiter. Another British variation? Australia? Maybe New Zealand. I'm an expert on inflections—the one practical result of an English major and the four speech courses I took to get rid of my Southern accent.

Paula's voice is softer now. Next will come the lemon twist and three onions on a plastic pick. She can't settle down! When I drank, the biggest olive, just one, was enough.

"What's on your mind?" she asks.

"Asparagus."

The waiter hovers. You can smell the lemon oil, and it cheers me up. "Remember the asparagus patch separating our yards? Better than a fence." I light a cigar, waiting for my own lemon, a whole one to drench the asparagus.

"Cuba, by way of Canada," Paula remembers. "He was an interlude, huh?"

"Eat," I say, finally. And she does. My asparagus. Parboiled. Still bright green. I remember the haze of our asparagus patch and every martini I ever drank. I remember Paula's clothesline and how her underwear looked after a summer shower. I remember too the day her husband left. It was five in the afternoon when she opened the door to the basement to bring up the blackberry preserves we had canned the day before.

On the phone, she listed each horror. His arms. His tongue. The cord. "I've got to read," she added, her words as foreign as if she were in Tibet. When I slammed her screen door, Plath and Arbus and Woolf and Dylan Thomas were in her lap, and her fingers were deformed with rage.

I sat there while the doctor put a needle in her arm, long after the sergeant had left and was drinking somewhere with his buddies trying to explain what business a widow had reading the first lines of four hardback books, over and over, aloud, when he was trying to make sense of a dead body and write it down before the shift changed.

"The insurance don't pay on one of these." I can still hear his country voice as he looked at the row of canned blackberries where Paula smashed them with a broomstick, the sticky pieces of glass embedded in the book covers. Ruined.

Dylan Thomas didn't live to see forty, but the bloated Welsh poet had more in common with those women than anybody wants to admit, and he wasn't the youngest. Plath was. Gas is painless. So is drowning with stones in your pocket. And I forget what happened to Arbus. I couldn't get past those eerie twins on the cover of her glossy photographs or Mae West preserved and powdered at seventy-plus, thinking peroxide equals sex. Frozen. Arbus froze me, and if she died, it was a relief. Tortured. She and Dylan Thomas and Paula's husband and the rest.

Nothing is what is left, and Paula pretends Russian vodka and funky pants make Saturday afternoons better than paraffin dripping on the blackest of berries in fifty half-pint jars!

A few facts. Yesterday I hit a display case with a hammer. A silver brooch turned to mint jelly and passed through a rack of lamb—still shiny, a hundred dollars' worth—heavy enough to hold onto. Dreams are like that. Anything can happen, and eventually you wake up. One more thing. Mint jelly is dyed apple, unless you pay a fortune for it at A Southern Season. I'd rather have a hamburger at Hardee's. Sometimes, there, men who look like *Deliverance* size you up. Sometimes the trash bins overflow, but it's all clear. A statement. Unfashionable.

The Philco radio ended up in my mother's basement, and I worked my way up. So did Paula. You can't do that in Great Britain where inflections still mean something. I don't know about Vienna. I've never been there.

The Other Woman

When I was in college, I played chess with a man who wanted to be a doctor. He didn't care what kind. He was tall and handsome, and he liked women. He had one for every occasion. A brown-skinned girl with talent and ambition for winter afternoons at the library and overnights when his roommate took the weekend off. The ambitious girl wrote poetry in French and spent the summers at Middlebury on a scholarship. She was good in bed and full of unexpected descriptions to go along with the requisite screams. Too busy, though, to notice he also had a light-skinned piece of fluff to show off at frat parties. I was the pal who made him laugh and was too scared to be seduced. He didn't try very hard. Like I say, he preferred compartments and predictability and long-range goals.

Then there was the woman he married. A physician's daughter with a steady job and a small inheritance. Plain and shrewd and black, she stayed close to home—a mansion on Chicago Boulevard that masked cold weather economies to the maids who stood in the gray slush of a customary Detroit winter waiting for the bus at the corner of Woodward Avenue. The physician's daughter knew all about trade-offs and the caste system.

The poet and I were friends. My chess partner didn't know that. It was a city university, and the dorm was the seventh floor of an old hotel. Students came from South America and south Georgia, and the few who could afford typewriters paid no attention to LIGHTS OUT. Curfew was a joke, and we had to look hard to find real boundaries.

The poet and I first met in the tub room the week she recovered from pneumonia. Naked, smeared with Vicks salve, she leaned against the chipped porcelain, a soggy copy of *The Heart Is a Lonely Hunter* in her hand, her hair hidden behind a bathing cap: "I can't believe Carson McCullers comes from my hometown and she's only twenty-one! See what you think." She ripped the novel in half and rested a minute before she handed me the first hundred pages.

I spent the rest of the night with my legs swung over a vinyl armchair behind the proctor's desk, safe in the perfect structure and searing words that seemed far away from this city block where, toward morning, the vice squad emerged from a black Buick to check the ID of the last reckless student sneaking in the revolving door. They wore porkpie hats and drank their coffee, free, at the S & C Diner in back of the hotel. Paradise Valley was a few blocks away on the other side of Woodward, and the Hancock station was close enough to generate tales of bashings and beatings and regular roundups of the women from the Valley. The city was new to me, and I spent a lot of time at the Detroit Institute of Arts looking at those murals and wondering how I could reconcile that Henry Ford was the one who saved my father from the WPA. By the time I majored in history and learned about Freda and Diego and revolution and art and the difference between grand and grandiosity, I had Henry and Father Coughlin in the same frightening category where their hate and power put the vice squad in a different perspective. Small men. It was a matter of imagery: the Hancock station, the Shrine of the Little Flower, and the Ford Mansions in Grosse Pointe.

Our dorm was crowded. Gossip drifted by in whispers through the hall and opened doors. A rumored ex-marine lived across from me, and she had propositioned three of my friends. Anna, the asthmatic maid, came from Warsaw where her brothers and sisters were buried. The housemother had been an artist's mistress before she saw the light and the economy and flew through nursing school into this niche. We studied ethics and wondered why someone didn't stop our philosophy professor, a senile man with a cane and a rambling speech on Marilyn Monroe instead of a final exam.

In the spring we found out the chess enthusiast cheated, on a regular basis, in his German class. Eventually we became privy to his line: a memorized imitation of courtliness and his respect for our minds. I've forgotten exactly what he said, but I remember how shocked we were that a doctor-to-be would cheat in German.

The poet and I stood in the stairwell in our slips, sharing a Pall Mall at midnight—promising each other that no man would ever touch our friendship. We were determined to marry. It was 1959.

I am a chronic liar about missing work and reporting charity donations on my income tax when there are none. She once stole a sirloin steak from Kroger's. "Hungry," she said. "Petty," I added. It's easy to forgive yourself. We thought scholarship was pure. Apart from life.

The talented brown-skinned girl married a union leader and stopped writing poetry. Her husband talked a lot about ethics and politics and Walter Reuther's 1933 itinerary through Europe, lofty talk that had nothing to do with black lunch pails and Labor Day parades. Her husband didn't have to cheat in German. I got married too, and we were in and out of each other's houses for the next twenty years. My husband became a lawyer eventually, but his time was limited and he never went to frat parties or invented hopeless love affairs to entice me. He was genuine to a fault.

I don't know what all this means. I wish I did. I'm older now, and my friend who stopped writing poetry but wrote YFA (your friend always) on her letters to me—through her honeymoon in Paris on misdirected union funds and my trips to the asylum—doesn't live on Riverside Drive anymore; and I can't find her number in the Manhattan directory.

German is an impossible language. It's best confined to Lily Marlene in the smoky cafés of Marlene Dietrich movies or "Liebling" whispered, over and over, in the corridors of my dreams. Now I understand why my chess partner would do most anything to become a doctor and why one woman couldn't satisfy him. He knew himself better than we knew him or ourselves. I, for example, thought I'd be happy with a clear conscience and a college degree.

Still in Kansas City

I'm a sucker for stories. It started with my mother and bedtime and ended with a guy who never got over his childhood. He should have been an actor and done something with all those words, but he ended up entertaining me. In bed and out. His face flies through my dreams and turns up on my ceiling; and I try to get over him. It's hard to forget last summer when I leaned back and listened, when heat was something to bypass, when the petunias outside my bedroom window browned and died before the July fireworks. It was a summer of rhetoric. The Democrats came to town. Flags waved and hopes were high. Cicely Tyson marched with the mayor up Auburn Avenue; and Atlanta was full of black art and black artists and parties that felt right. The first weekend in August we bought a ceiling fan and laid in a supply of gin. The curtains blew out the window and Howie kept on talking.

Howard Renaldo. He captured me. Howie was fond of my feet, so I took off my shoes. My hair got in our way, so I shaved my head. Howie wore a diamond in one ear—like a chip from a star. I followed suit. Picture us in our underwear under his family photograph, framed in gilt, taken the October before his father died. Picture us in a room with a rococo coffee table and no chairs: resting in a corner, laughing at the messages on his machine, ignoring the doorbell, laughing until we hurt bad, in that place under our ribs where hysteria shows. Breathless. The two of us.

Here is the New South and outside the city limits— Georgia, still. I grew up in the Midwest. Chicago is a cage. Twenty-one before I met a Christian, but I got out without anyone sitting Shiva. No matter where you go, there's a look and a protocol; and here things are no different.

That's why Howie's place appealed to me. Once I shut his door, I could forget my family and the ten years I spent trying to teach school in the Windy City. Once I clicked that dead bolt, I could cancel out anything colored pink or khaki. The Spot and Peachtree Cafe and Otto's and the man who owns all three, forgotten. Lenox Square and Phipps Plaza, forgotten. Yes, the immediate and the far away retreated as I waited in Howie's apartment.

The people Howie talked about wore clothes, I'm sure; but he wove his stories around their wisecracks while I relaxed and invented my own imagery. It suited us until, little by little, the stories of my mother took over. I listened—anticipating facts, in their own good time, would clear the air—like the rainstorm we thought would come soon.

"Light those candles," Howie said, digging out the wicks with a table knife, "and if we can't pay the rent, we'll burn the place down."

I came to Atlanta with my head full of failure. Ten years teaching under the gun for a department head who played cribbage with the navy blue policeman hired to keep the halls safe from everything. They staked out the boiler room, filling it with smoke and big city angst, while hoodlums set up business in the hallways, as if by invitation. When revolution finally came, the department head and the cop retired to their respective saloons and watched the protestors on TV telling the truth to reporters whose fondness for precise diction and the pause congealed into icy objectivity.

I taught across the hall from a woman who screwed a rock star on her lunch hour. She lived around the corner in a high-rise and in no time developed a bladder infection that made her itch and burn and try to forget about sex. The female anatomy will only take so much pressure.

Teachers are strange. The counselor who alphabetized A through Gh spent her lunch hour wiping doorknobs with a white handkerchief. Nobody dared ask her why. The football coach, a large man who was convinced that the varsity's rules were his too, was said to have a list of senior girls in his breast pocket along with a red pen to keep track of his score.

Mine is a nineteenth-century prologue. The spinster. Preoccupied. Distracted. The school system. Deficiencies. Needs no one could meet, yet I burrowed into my job and hoped it would save me. Last winter I walked along Lake Shore Drive, glad the snow and wind could still penetrate the scarf I wrapped around my mouth. Sometimes I imagined the football coach had added me to his list.

Every Friday at four, the teacher across the hall (her name was Geraldine) pulled me away from my grade book and averages, and we walked to the nearest tavern where we ordered up and watched the lights flash on the pinball machine. Her rock star was replaced by the basketball coach—after the rock star's wife called from L.A. and announced the color of Geraldine's eyes and the size of her bra—one November Thursday, long after midnight.

"He always goes for the same color and size." The wife's voice was shrill.

"Apparently he leaves their phone numbers in his pockets, too," I prodded Geraldine, appalled at his predictability and her unpaid medical bills. The basketball coach was married too; but he left the senior girls alone and settled for Saturday afternoons with Geraldine.

"A step up." I tried for optimism.

"Other people's patterns are easy to spot." Geraldine laid her glasses on the table, and we ordered another round. After a week of ducking in and out of restless study halls, an early start on Friday night was about all I expected from life. You could see the snow, outside the windows, thick and steady enough to make cabs unsafe if we stayed past supper.

Sooner or later, the conversation got around to our families. But we spoke in shorthand—avoiding the truth by condensing it. Geraldine talked the most. I tried to make connections. It's the same with Howie. He'll never tire of talking about his father in his heyday, sitting at Toots Shore's on a Friday night, but he moves from there to his father's funeral and he tells who came out of hiding to attend; how the wake spilled out on Fifth Avenue; every detail down to the lace on the priest's cuffs. Yes, the sunshine in Atlanta and Howie's New York memories eventually replaced Chicago's Friday afternoon gloom and bar conversation.

May I present Howie's favorite Friday story, then, secondhand, in his father's voice?

We would meet on Friday no matter where we'd been during the week; and Toots would come to our table and take the order. The best prime and the house red. On this particular Friday after we had finished the meal, one of the men, new to the table, called Toots back over.

"How'd you like your steak?" Toots lit a cigar.

"Well, it was nothing like the steak I had this week in Kansas City."

Toots looked at the silverware for a minute, his match in the ashtray; then he said, "Well, just remember this—if you go again—after you finish your steak, no matter how good it is, you'll still be in Kansas City."

Howie follows up fast: "They're all dead now. Toots. The creep. My father."

I have trouble imagining that particular man's scene. Hollywood and New York. Vienna. London. South America. Movies must be distributed. And the men at that table distributed them. Now Woody Allen fights against coloring the black-and-white images of Howie's father's world and saves its stylized kisses from burning red.

Before he died, Howie's father told the Kansas City story, again and again, to the Puerto Rican doorman who sits in the lobby of his building on Central Park West.

"My father was a handsome man with a full head of gray hair and straight shoulders," says Howie. His voice cracks with regret.

Unlike Howie I kept my stories to myself. It was a family tradition; and I got my imagery from Vanessa Redgrave's face and the speeding trains on TV specials. The words came from my mother. Somewhere inside herself—the stories weren't planned, they escaped. We are Hungarian Jews who read Elie Wiesel and Primo Levi and nod our heads. Jews who paid our taxes and couldn't believe we would be taken. My mother's accent remains. "Nine jobs . . . three thousand came to clear the trees for an airfield . . . the trees fell, I dug the ditch, a forest on one side . . . we lived in a prison and the other prisoners were old, in chains; and then *they came and took us to another place.*"

I woke up this morning with the worries of the night stuck in my eyes, leaning on the shower stall, waiting for the hot and cold to mix. I take my vitamin tablet then with a handful of tap water, naked. Today the pill stuck, so I had to cough it loose before the water touched me. More awake than I wanted to be.

I wish I'd known Howie's father because he was connected to things and he had a place, a part to play; and it sustained him. Last Friday, I cut up a rabbit while Howie was collecting rents. I thought about hunters and bird dogs. Old Southern preoccupations. The pink flesh lay on the counter while I covered it with pepper. The rabbit's muscles looked white in the fluorescent glare— the color of dental floss. Howie and I remain stuck in our own history—though we have forsaken our respective Friday nights and Sunday mornings and tried to wedge ourselves in this empty room.

Howie was in no hurry to change anything, and he didn't care where or if I worked. Sex may explain his laissez-faire attitude; but it wasn't my body or our romance that he needed. Just my attention turned toward him. Unwavering.

Eventually I had to get a job. An outstanding superintendent of schools arrived in Atlanta from Brooklyn; so I filled out an application and waited. I was put on a waiting list, and I continued waiting. Then I graded papers for a testing service until it closed down. Another matter of alleged connections and shady deals. I had time to consider Howie's investments and mine as well.

The day I had my head shaved, I thought of my mother in the camps. How she missed the feel of her hair in the wind. The luxury when she was able to eat again. And here I was making changes in the name of freedom that she will never understand. Oh, she might like the story of Howie's father because she likes old movies and porterhouse steaks; and the corruption in Howie's family can't hold a candle to what she's left behind, can't compare to a week's worth of Chicago headlines. My mother reads Saul Bellow and wanders through museums and grieves for a city that seemed to be headed in a better direction until the mayor dropped dead in his tracks.

On Labor Day, we planned a picnic. Indoors, of course, and we began with a bottle of Bombay gin—getting into an argument over the picture on the label before we had the first drink. Howie dreamed up a crazy story about Queen Victoria; and I believed him. Howie called me his stooge. A delightful stooge, he explained. A term of contempt? Or endearment? How was I to know? There are people, like Elizabeth Taylor, who hurt all the time; and little meannesses rise like bubbles from their lips because their pain is never going to end. They keep their nastiness to themselves day and night; only these bubbles give you some idea what the unspoken truth is. That's why I left Howie. I couldn't bear his loss stalking me too. I couldn't add his life to mine.

Before it was over, the Baltimore Catechism and its "Near Occasions of Sin" dominated us, for Howie is still a Catholic and a provincial one at that; and I could not merge with his chosen words—not ever.

My mother's story. My mother's geography. My mother's advice. All of it resurfaced one September afternoon when Howie proclaimed his disgust for bargaining, his contempt for *haggling.* He was a breath away from *Jew you down;* and we both knew it. It came down to a warning my mother had bequeathed to me: "If you lose those who will defend you, then you are lost indeed."

What has Howie done with himself since last summer? He ran the Peachtree in record time. He invested in another duplex and he rings me up on the weekends to complain about some out-of-town property he bought on a floodplain. But, if I know Howie, they'll run a freeway over it and he'll cash in. What about me? I have moved to

Midtown and am raking leaves with an industry I didn't know I possessed. The new superintendent finally called me for an interview, and I'm trying to find my balance within the city limits.

Near Occasions of Sin

1: Peggy

I got up, after spitting the revolting wetness in a towel, and walked across the room. There, covered by the missing sheet, I watched the sun come up over the white marble building that separated the campus from a slum, already scheduled to be torn down.

A dwarfed cherry tree and a narrow strip of grass stood between the Detroit Institute of Arts and the sidewalk. A cab passed while I sat staring at the bus-stop sign, conscious of my body. A breeze moved the curtains; sweat dripped down my back. The last ice tray sat on the floor, full and melting, next to a pile of pillows.

Relaxing my arms, I let the sheet fall and slowly rubbed myself. My eyes searched the wall for a picture, a bookcase, some evidence of Harvey's personality. But all he had were the usual shirts from the cleaners and a picture of the football team from Duke University. He wasn't even in it. Across the room on the mattress, Harvey lay snoring.

"Relax, Peggy." He eventually sat up and ignored what I was doing. "I know a guy who works in room service at the Sheraton. How 'bout a pitcher of juice?"

I nodded. He pulled on his jeans without bothering with jockey shorts, and before I could find my voice, he was out the door. I watched his sandals on the cement as he ran under the window and across the street. The hotel canopy was around the corner.

I bolted to the shower, turned the hot and cold handles, and stood still. I lathered Dial into my hair. The water was too hot.

A stack of washcloths lay on the floor outside the stall. I tried to dry my hair enough to pin it up. No mirror, no bath towels. My slip lay across Harvey's Eames chair. I pulled it over my head and walked back to the window to wait. Some dead bugs and a broken cigarette lighter on the dusty sill. I was already sweating.

Soon Harvey came into view carrying a cardboard box and a sack. "Buzz." I answered with the button on the wall. In seconds, we met at the door. He set the packages on the floor and picked me up. "Hey, hcy . . . how can we?" His hands were under me, my slip far above my knees.

He moved around the room, grabbing and picking up, kicking one pillow into another one the same size and color. The pillows behind my head, he lay beside me, whispering so low I couldn't put the sounds together. Then he moved down until his face was over my stomach.

I watched. It seemed slow and fast at the same time. I lay back and my voice was hoarse.

We drank orange juice out of a jelly glass. My nipples held the excitement, the wildness of the night, and I could hear myself asking him for things I barely knew the names of. And he was doing them in dreamy, slow motion, one hand behind his head, his face against my cheek.

How can anyone be shy after the words that passed through the heat of that morning? We turned up the record player so loud that bus passengers heard it and looked up. We laughed at them and fell asleep without a thought of ice or gin. The music full blast, and no fan.

Sunday night we walked two blocks to a Japanese restaurant where the air-conditioning made us shake. Next, we stopped at the drugstore for the necessities. I stood in the phone booth waiting for the phone to ring back at the dorm. I have always been a liar. "Angie, tell them I'm staying home for a funeral Monday!"

"Whose funeral?" Angie is never going to get a scholarship.

"You remember my aunt?"

"Peggy, have you lost your mind? Your aunt died last year, and you cried for a week."

"Well, all the better. Keep those details in your head,

and if the housemother asks you any questions, give her
the full story. She'll cut you off in the middle anyway,
because all she cares about is her lousy job. Snow her!
And worry about the truth when you get to philosophy
class. You might just pass if you stay on my good side
and pull this one off!"

"Peggy, answer me one question. Are you drinking again?"

"Yes, I just finished sipping sake with Harvey in an air-
conditioned room, but I have more important things on
my mind now. And when they're over, he's taking me to
Baker's Keyboard Lounge."

2: Peggy

"Stay away from near occasions of sin," Rose told her
friend Peggy in the toy department at Saks Fifth Avenue.
They were invited to the same party, and Rose wasn't
going. It was Christmas Eve. "What do you think I'm
doing right now?" Peggy hurried through polar bears to
teddies and grabbed two. At the gift wrap, the two women
were silent. Peggy concentrated on her red nail polish.
"I'll take the velvet bows," she said.

Snow fell in the street in front of the General Motors
building, and cabs were everywhere. Sinatra was billed
as *Pal Joey* and the Salvation Army had not given up yet.
"I'm looking for a tea room," Peggy winked, rounding the
corner of I. Magnin. "Will that satisfy you?"

There are no tea rooms in Detroit, and they both knew
it. They turned the corner and walked into a narrow cof-
fee shop with green plastic leaves and dimmed lights.
"Little Drummer Boy" made the space between them full.
Two drunks were extolling the virtues of the Teamster's
Union to the counterman.

Peggy continued: "Do you expect me to spend the rest
of my life in the shower or shoveling snow? Take away
parties and weddings and a little scotch after supper,
and what's left? Do you think my job is a challenge?"

"It wouldn't hurt you to crawl out of your apartment

and breathe some fresh air, Peggy. Have you thought about skiing?"

"What do you think they do at Boyne Mountain in the evenings? Fade away with Swiss chocolate?" Peggy's sling-backs are edged in salt. She stares at them.

"Unless you want to end up as bar conversation, you better go easy on your smart-ass routine and lay off the whiskey. By the time the sun goes down, you're blistered. You haven't been to Mass before noon in five years. I take it back. After Johnny Kwitkowski got married, you showed up at six and then went to bed. Let's not talk about that fiasco!"

"Maybe I'll change jobs, Rose. Become a gopher for the Catholic Youth Organization. Crochet lace doilies? Bake nut bread? That stupid sister of mine gets through the day on cinnamon rolls, and she makes them herself. Is that wholesome enough for you?"

It was 5:00 P.M. "Maybe I'll stay here for the rest of the evening. 'Course I'll miss Santa Claus and your husband drinking Vernor's ginger ale. Take these teddy bears and go home to what you know best!"

"Sit down, Peggy. I'm not leaving you. It's just that catechism got me through. Nobody survives alone. It's OK if you leave me. Pay some attention to your family. Go home for Sunday dinner. You might surprise yourself and like it."

"Catechism? It's easy not to commit murder and stay out of married men's beds. I'm never that angry," said Peggy as she pulled a hangnail to the quick. "It's the other list. Venial sin. I go through the gamut every other day. Lust? Rage? Presumption and despair? Are they connected like building blocks? Father Donnelly recognizes my voice, and it's not funny anymore.

"Live long enough, and you'll be fed up with everything. 'Honor thy father and mother'? Mortal sin for sure. And if everybody did it, dangerous. The best thing is to run. Brave people disappear. Postpone. There's a lot to be said for working late and pulling the phone cord at strategic times. Stay the hell away, or you're a dead duck.

Have you ever seen a dead duck? I have, and the feathers and blood don't leave you. My parents fight all the time. No claws. Just enough rage to bury us all!

"I'd like to r-e-l-a-x. Is that so much to ask? Angie told me when you get Demerol, right before they wheel you in, it's better than relaxing. Well, I won't go that route to get there. I saw her hemorrhaging in the toilet after her first baby. Tucks and an empty bottle of Tylenol #3. The doctor told her if she needed more pain medicine, she shouldn't be going home. Her husband told her the insurance didn't cover an extra day. Angie was in a sweat, and those green eyes of hers aren't pretty anymore.

"How about it, Rose? I suffered enough for twenty-five years. I'm not ordering up a second helping on a cracked plate. A husband and babies? Don't hand me that nice girl crap! Where are the nice boys? Screwing each other at the Brass Rail? Playing first cello in the symphony? Laying a mannequin at Saks? If anybody around here told the truth, I'd faint dead away. Priests aren't the only liars.

"I think I'm getting an ulcer from my job. A bleeding ulcer. My brains are bleeding too. Nothing is fastened in my head, and I'm sick of your goddamned advice!" Rose was speechless. The counterman looked up.

"When I was growing up, we had a truck farm but no truck. There was a job for all of us, including my mother. I got up early to pick cucumbers before the heat of the day—bushels of them. You crawl around the vines, and pickers turn your hands black. I hate my father. He taught me more than anybody needed to know about work in that garden. I'm an expert on rotten tomatoes and those pale green worms that eat holes in them before they rot. I know a few things about corn borers too. Green peppers aren't bad. They're light and shiny and easy to pick, but they don't sell good, so it doesn't pay to plant a whole row.

"I liked the end of the season best. When you couldn't get people to pick it for nothing, and you were left with the weeds to plow under. Practicing law wasn't enough. We had to save. We wore hand-me-downs so we could move to the right address. Did you ever hear Randy Newman's song about burning down the cornfield? He's a genius!

"Do you think I live downtown by accident? My parents hate this neighborhood. They think fire will break out, or the elevator will stick any minute. Do you know something? I don't care. I'd like to hole up on the fourteenth floor and count the cars in that gray slush on Beaubien. The kitchen here is the size of a postage stamp with appliances to match and no windows. I can stand in the middle and reach everything: olives, ice. . . .

"The lights on the freeway? The freighters on the river? I'm above it all. Oh, sometimes I miss Christmas Eve Communion. But I have my own candles. Blue spruce is available too, for a price. You have to say good-bye to your childhood, sooner or later.

"I was coming out of Lou Walker's last week when I saw a kid I grew up with, Eugene Cataldo. He memorized every batting average in the American League. Our whole family loved him. His older brother was shell-shocked. His sister drank from sixteen on—that was after the beatings. His mother never drove a car in her life, and they had money. 'How's that W-O-N-D-E-R-F-U-L father of yours?' I said. Don't hand me that shit about big families and the old neighborhood!

"I may drink myself unconscious once a month, but nobody beats me up, and I buy my suits in those new shops on Livernois and Seven Mile Road. Your mistake is you expect more. Wake up, Rose. It's not the Middle Ages!

"Sin is everywhere, and the only hell is right here in town: on the streetcar and in that locked ward at Receiving Hospital where they put the heroin addicts and the botched suicides. I spent the night there once with my eyes wide open. A fat psychiatrist with a cigar to match had a few words for me, but the priests stay out of there, and you better believe it's a near occasion of sin. The toilets don't flush, and sometimes an IV screws up before they unlock the door. They put a sheet over the body, and the whores shut their foul mouths for at least three minutes. You have time to consider a few possibilities.

"Gloria Steinem knows what life is like. You don't see her in anybody's kitchen! Toledo is a lot like Detroit, and her mother's name was Ruth. Psychotic. At home. Gloria did the dirty work after her tap lessons. Her year in India? Smith? She wasn't fooled by travel and the East Coast preppies. Don't get me wrong. I'm not a feminist. But I'm not a damn fool, either."

3: Rose

"Rose, like the flower," I said slowly and waited. Just what I need: a plumber who can't speak English, I thought, as I looked straight at his black eyes and fingernails. He carried a handful of corroded pipes, and his hair hung over one eye.

We have been taking showers in cold water for three days, and frankly, it doesn't take much more to destroy a marriage. Why is it we always blame each other? Not for the problem. For what goes with it. "Where are the handkerchiefs, Rose," my husband says, looking through a pile of clean laundry. "Goddamn it, Rose, what do you do all day?" The sun comes in the window, and dust settles on the floor.

He's gone now, and I'm getting ready for the tub. I intend to drown myself in lavender bath oil and worry about whether it rains. I like to sleep when it rains. I like to read too, but I've run out. The library keeps crazy hours, and the fines are impossible. If I had what I'd paid in lost books, we could spend a week in Venezuela!

My friends all travel. They mail postcards from Hong Kong and Martinique. They bring home flimsy clothes and pictures no bigger than a three by five card. As long as it packs. . . .

My best friend Peggy spend the winter in Ireland and brought back some whiskey from the Shannon Airport. She told me, "It rained most of the time." She was living with a man ten years younger with a brogue that could

carry her off to sleep. She came home with a pile of old
New Yorkers and has taken to reading Edna O'Brien. She
could have stayed right here for that. She also brought a
bottle of calcium pills, and now she drinks hot milk at
parties.

I'll never figure Peggy out. She was my best friend in
college, and the summer I got married she had an affair
with a piano player who liked lab alcohol with his orange
juice. He was nearsighted, and he nearly fractured my
copy of Dylan Thomas as he read it to her in bed. He was
up at six in the morning and, if one of us didn't stop
him, at the piano with some German lieder. Baby fat and
baby face and blue eyes that would break your heart!
Well, he did. He had a little honey in the Chemistry Department too. A piano is easy to find if you're out to
serenade the world.

I like the automobile business. People don't expect
much in the way of humanity, and I have always been
good with numbers. We got in on the ground floor, Peggy
and I, and we both moved around a little but stayed in
the same building. We have lunch together every day.

"This is going too far." I watched her order a milk shake
when the waitress came around for our drinks.

"You have to think about the future." Peggy winked. If I
didn't know better, I'd think she was pregnant. I can't
imagine what that Irishman told her. She is not unhappy.
In fact, she has a date tonight with a married man who
has been on her floor for six weeks. Moved here to get
away from the Chicago winters, he says. Does he think a
ten-degree hike in temperature will make a difference?
Nobody moves to Detroit anymore. Henry Ford is dead,
and Iacocca is just a flash in the pan.

Peggy and I never talk about sex. I just watch her year
after year and wonder where the hell it will all end. May
God forgive me! Nowhere, I guess. This new man has a
deaf daughter and a beautiful wife. Put that together
with Peggy and make sense of it if you can!

I still have my copy of Dylan Thomas and the dress I
got married in. It was thin cotton with an eyelet bodice.

My mother made it, and I thought it was the whitest
material on the bolt at J. L. Hudson's. I have never been
partial to silk.

4: Peggy

I saw Harvey again hurrying across the lawn at Rose's
with a custom-made blue blazer covering what he ate
since those weekends when he made me scream half the
night. What made me swallow his stories? Fifteen years
had passed; his wife was dead. An auto wreck. None of
those lingering things that grow out of the menopause.
D.O.A. Did he change? I fancied that sinecure and the
property tucked away at the lake made him happy. He
said it did. A few weekends in my bed scrapped that story.

He still had his accent and the right words whispered
over and over, and he told me, "Gray hair is becomin'."

Becoming what? I thought. It's hard to argue when the
bedroom walls turn into a cave and you are so liquored
up (his words) you forget priests and dago red and what's
happened to your breasts in the years between.

Well, I traded one set of bastards for another. And
nobody pushed me into it. He had that woman all along,
all those years, and he knows more about the Mafia than
my father dare admit. Some trade-off I made! A lawyer for
a con! Ethan Allen for an Eames chair!

We took his daughter to the zoo, went to her recitals at
Cranbrook, and fried chicken in my kitchen. "Where do
you keep the paper towels, Peggy?" Where did I keep my
life until he came back? I kept my body on hold because
nobody knew what to do with it.

We were fastened together that whole summer, my last
year of school, when I finally kissed Angie good-bye and
moved in. I brought my makeup bag and a leather suitcase. I left my plaid skirts and cashmeres in my old
bedroom at home. Southerners are formal on the outside,
and I always looked good in black. My mother cried, and
my father threatened things I'd rather not repeat.

By August we couldn't sleep in that apartment, even with a fan. We did it on the beach at Belle Isle before the place got dangerous, we did it in the shower, and he steamed away my brains. I read a lot of Russian history in that Eames chair. I don't mind saying I was naked most of the time, and summer turned to winter, and I bought a blue satin comforter. It felt like what I wanted. The pipes knocked, and the halls smelled like bacon or diapers, depending on the day of the week. The Lullaby Diaper man and the trumpet player who lived upstairs were the only men I saw besides my professors.

"Peggy, you look worn out," my French instructor told me.

"I think I may have mono," I lied. My mother bought me a fur coat for Christmas, and we laid it on the floor and ruined the lining on New Year's Eve. My grades didn't suffer. I had lots of time while he was at those meetings, and I loved waiting for him.

"A bloodless bastard," Rose told me. And, finally, I took a plane to Hartford to visit my sister in May.

Her gin was the right brand, and it came by the gallon. My sister thinks her pelvis is sacred, and she has a housekeeper who never lets her see reality. The children don't look Italian; they look good. Harvey never called me. I didn't leave a letter, but he knew.

Anyway, this time Harvey surrounded me. Rose's party stretched into two weeks in Italy. He watched me paint my toenails in bed and then locked the door.

"It'll take a truck to move your books," Harvey said.

"So get one." I wear reading glasses now, and a cami-sole to cover my stomach scar.

"Elisa, let's get on with these dates. The world didn't arrive yesterday and that school you go to can disappear fast if you don't work hard." She means a lot to me. I had one too many abortions. A butcher on Dexter. Elisa seems like a bonus. She has those same Southern manners, and they get me every time.

Harvey didn't lose his touch, either. "My nurse taught me, and I like women," he's fond of reminding me. Old ladies, those unmarried spectres who flit around midtown bookstores, even bag ladies. Harvey gives road directions, as if it mattered. How he ever came to this town puzzled me at first. I know the whole South moved here to get on the assembly line, but he was never poor. He says it was relatives. And I used to believe him. Not anymore. He doesn't have the truth in him. He gave my mother some high-priced Italian wine and waxed forth on Luigi Barzini for a full twenty minutes the first time I brought him home. My father was harder to handle and, in the end, we gave up trying. It felt good to breathe some air and hear a different set of plans. And Harvey had 'em. He also had connections and hands that made me shake.

He had been raised by maids, and his idea of cleaning up was to sweep the laundry into a corner. I wasn't much better. So we kept it simple and every month his sister's cleaning woman came over and told me how hopeless men were. She was old and wise, and I should have known she wasn't talking about paychecks. I made tea and watched her work. She brought her own equipment and left us the broom. "You are a caution too," she said. I gave her a bottle of Canadian Club for Christmas, and she brought us a little wooden Jesus her grandson had painted. I left the church behind me, but we hung the ornament on the window shade and played Sinatra's "I'll Be Home for Christmas" before we left for dinner. Five courses and a French menu. His legs were never far from mine. But he was off to one of those meetings before the pastry tray arrived. He left a big tip, and the waiter was glad to call me a cab. I can't stomach politics, never thought it made a difference. I heard enough bullshit at the dinner table growing up to last me a lifetime, and you can crash all that china and crystal for brides to the floor. I prefer paper plates.

5: Peggy

I feel old and adrift. My body longs for someone to take over who knows what he's doing. I'd like to crawl away from my life and hug Harvey forever. Any bedroom would do, but I prefer the Ritz. In the winter Boston is all lights and snowflakes, and you can see the Common out the window of the Ritz bar. Harvey doesn't care, but history means something. Sylvia Plath and Anne Sexton sat there after Robert Lowell's poetry class and made plans. I won't wallow in that kind of despair, but the place fills my dreams. The thinnest brandy snifters! And they don't run out of Courvoisier!

I can't help but believe those Irish pubs would do something for my spirit too, and they are right up Harvey's alley.

I bought some leather boots last week, and my old winter coat will still take the wind off the ocean. I just pull my mink collar up and make sure there's an extra pair of gloves in my bag. You must be ready for a few emergencies. There's another thing we agree on, and Harvey has a wad of bills for his part. He's old-fashioned about a lot of things, and if I were a fool, I'd think he was gallant. But I wasn't raised Catholic for nothing. Form and substance are not the same.

I packed a few books today and looked around for my red nail polish. Harvey can put me to sleep, but I get up at night like an alarm, even with him. It helps to have something to read.

I didn't need the gloves, but there were a few emergencies. We circled the airport for two hours, and both of us felt the pull of collapse. There's something about middle age that people don't talk about, and I'm no exception. Harvey held my hand and asked the stewardess for those little pillows and another blanket. I didn't have to tell him how scared I was, and he didn't let go.

Then he shocked me. It was four in the afternoon and snowing so hard we could barely see our boots, but he walked me over to Saks and bought one of those double-duty coats with a pull-out fur lining and a hood. On the elevator, going down, he mashed me against the wall and ruined my lipstick. It was not his public personality.

We walked to the Ritz, and Harvey ordered tea sent up. I took a scalding bath and came out of the bathroom as he was pouring it. "Tea, Harvey? Have you turned into a Puritan?" But I knew what he felt too. I snuggled up in his robe and we sat by the window and watched the snow hit the apartment roofs across the street. "Get out of that suit. You'll get pneumonia!"

We ate a late supper in bed. It was still snowing at 3:00 A.M., and you could see the lights on the snowplows far below. The next morning Harvey met his cronies for breakfast at Friendley's and I stayed in bed watching Jane Pauley pretend she knows something besides how to modulate her lovely voice. That's about as much TV as I can stand, so I got up and took out a black wool dress with long sleeves and pinned up my hair.

"You look like an Italian countess," Harvey said.

More like a French whore, I thought, pulling up my stockings.

"You know the silver flask Rose and I joke about? I think it's time." He put his hat back on.

We saw one in the Hoffritz window, and he had my initials put in the center. He mailed one to Rose too, with silver polish and his business card. I was surprised, and Rose nearly shook his hand off the next time we came by her house.

"Who do you think you are? The Bobbsey Twins?" Harvey said.

6: Rose

I keep the monogrammed flask on the top laundry shelf. The day before I got pregnant again, leaning over a pile of bleached towels in the darkness of the laundry room— sudden and wild—I went to the fire station on Birchwood Road with my daughter's nursery-school class. We did the usual things, but what changed me forever was watching a short, pockmarked fireman explain his job and then hop on a ladder to show the kids what the air is like outside a burning building. They clapped till their hands were sore. Glory, that's what he has, I thought. I wanted some too. And, of all the things possible, it's what I am least likely to get.

"Martyrdom," if I play my cards down the middle. "Escape," if I find a Harvey to rescue me. "Oblivion," if I keep on drinking. Glory goes to football heroes and women who get Mother of the Year awards for surviving widowhood and five kids in a chintz apron with a row of canned pears on the countertop.

Peggy is never home now. Long weekends all the time. She tells me all about the cities and the bookstores, but I'm not stupid. They don't make words for the best part, and anyway Peggy wouldn't talk about it. There're things I won't tell her either, but they have nothing to do with the bedroom. I'm afraid if I start talking, I'll never stop. You've seen those boring women at office parties who feel they have a corner on misery. I almost pushed one down the stairs once, and I was stone sober.

"Oh, Peggy, it was all so different when our biggest problem was getting a 'Hold' off our grades for fifty dollars in library fines, and we thought the bad guy was your piano player who kept that borrowed stack of German lieder in his basement after you told him good-bye."

7: Rose

Things happen fast at the Sullivans'. First there was the snow. Then the accident. It didn't happen to me. My son told me about it: "It was a snowy day. The electric line was down. She didn't know where she was going. She lost one arm and a leg. Now she has a fake leg and a wheelchair. She goes to my school."

Then my son got mono. He kisses nobody. He's in a wheelchair too. Let's not go into that. He stayed home all day, a good patient. He likes chicken noodle soup and bakery pies. What more could you want? I talked him into some Bruce Springsteen instead of those educational TV shows. They must get dead bodies to try out for the teachers: a monotone and a stiff neck and a little below average on the Stanford-Binet. I poured some bourbon in my coffee and tried to warm up.

Then the water heater broke. It was six months old, and they sent out a new one, but the phone calls took the starch out of me. They put you on hold and play Muzak and then they "Yes, ma'am" you to death. I have a filthy mouth, and I'm afraid I'll let loose. The tension is too much.

Then nothing happened. I waited out the mono and watched him sleep. He has blond hair and brown eyelashes, and his cheeks are still soft. Mono could last through adolescence! There's only so much bourbon you can get away with. That's what bothers me. I can't figure out when this is going to end. "Take a walk," Peggy says. In this snow? I can count on her for some stupid advice. I took a nap instead. The quilts are old and soft, and so are the pillows. I like to look at the ads for leotards. Dance France, Barely Legal, Isotoners. Nobody wears Danskins anymore, and you can get leg warmers in every color.

In my dreams all the dancers are weighed down by their shoes; they struggle to move, and the heaviness comes through in the music too. They are dressed in bright red, and their eyes are on fire.

My oldest daughter works at the A & P bagging groceries. It's part of a special program with the county. She loves it. At twenty-two, her life is predictable, and she helps me with the dishes every night. The garbage slides off the plates, and the disposal takes care of it all. I used to worry about accidents. Not anymore.

8: Rose

Someone, an expert, said it is clinical. You know, it means more than it seems to mean. But it's his favorite color. He wore a purple leotard to Creative Movement class when he was five years old. My psychiatrist said, "He's too pretty; you're asking for it!" Will a black one make it better? The point, I guess, is don't bend him that way. He's copied my voice, my gestures, my exaggerations. But I put the leotard in the trash.

His bedroom has grayish ropelike wallpaper, a thick rust carpet, muted plaid spreads of blue and gray; but he still loves purple and he still sounds like me because I have been his companion all these scary years when I floundered, near death, with the color purple right behind my eyelids—out of reach.

The wheelchair came later, and what difference did it make then? He's safe now, enclosed with stainless steel and a modern motor. They call it multi-handicapped, and one part feeds another, and the collapse waits for the future. The tests don't stop unless you protest, and I do. There is plenty I don't want to know. I don't give a damn about research or those Junior League imitations with bubble haircuts who devote their Tuesdays to raising money for schools that look like a cross between a college campus and an English rose garden. Strip away that crap and at least you find the truth, and you have a few afternoons to watch the light fade on your porch glider and some money left to hire a gardener. I'm with Peggy—black dirt doesn't go with red nail polish, hers or mine.

Little by little, I'm looking at the whole picture, digging out the jargon and finding something for myself to go along with my rage. Josh Greenfield helps, and so does the Bible. In the middle of the night, my husband's shoulder, the ceiling fan, and the open window help the most.

I tried a support group once with a speaker. Support is something I thought went along with girdles and D-cup bras. I never use the word anymore. The speaker talked about the importance of teaching the child to set the table and loving him. I asked if that was all she could tell us from twenty years of special education and a big stack of notecards. She said I needed to do something about my hostility. The other mothers stared at me, and the school psychologist said, "I have a blind daughter in college."

I went home and kicked a hole in the bedroom wall. Thin plasterboard. My husband fixed it without saying a word. The support group makes a quilt together at Christmas, and that takes up a lot of time. They tell each other their sad stories, except for one mother, who is retarded, too. They are stumped by her, but she is good with a needle and bakes terrific brownies. Borderline. Pretty. I told Peggy she must make some man an ideal wife. Peggy laughed a little too long. I still can't believe she was married by a judge in his chambers without so much as a daffodil in sight.

9: Peggy

Harvey and I are sitting in black leather chairs in the corner of the Ponchartrain Wine Cellars. The Dom Perignon is finished. His cigar is lit. He is listening to me.

"The thing that meant the most to you was your cock. Now it doesn't work. Your troubles are over!" I begin. He has a prostitute from Brazil tucked away in Grosse Pointe, and he has just told me her breasts sag and her other parts are not as tight as they once were. I am forty years old. The rest is not important.

Harvey is talking to the waiter about champagne. Three weeks ago I met a man on the track. I'm a little near-sighted, but at six in the morning, who can see? He told me a few things and looked at my sweatband. He runs a six-minute mile.

I stay on level territory and take it a little at a time. The next day I bought a sports bra and got a haircut. I wear my husband's undershirt and gray sweats. I hate the brand name shit.

I am listening to myself. The waiter uncorks the bottle. My husband is in the men's room. I let the champagne sit. I am left with the roses and his cigar ashes. The man from the track is still on my mind. "This might be my last good screw. When I'm old I'll know it wasn't just anybody. I think I want this man, this runner. I'd like to climb on his lap without clothes and mash my face and body into his. I'd like to scream—not for help, either."

I look at my husband for one full minute. He concentrates on the cigar smoke. I lower my voice: "Harvey, I'll drag your ass across the street. Whether I get anything or not, the attorneys will!" Harvey takes his time with the pastry tray.

On the way home, the lights across the river do nothing for my spirit. The dashboard looks like a computer, and the radio is broken. It has been fixed three times. All that remains is static.

We have separate rooms. Our condo faces a golf course. I take lessons in the summer. There's not much breeze, but the trees are beautiful. A week ago I bought a vibrator. I hate to say this, but it doesn't work. They came in all sizes and covered a whole corner of the store. I was so stupid, I thought you needed a prescription. Not anymore. All this is new to me, but I learn fast.

Harvey's daughter sets the frying pan on the counter and burns out the element in the oven. Thank God, we don't have a microwave. "Stay out of the kitchen, Elisa; you're dangerous!" Next year she will be thirteen. I plan to buy her a diaphragm: "Try it out. You'll see. It's all bullshit, if the guy doesn't love you."

When I was a girl, we spent the summers at the lake waiting for my father. All I wanted was a little shade. There were five of us. My oldest sister's boyfriend had a big car and tight clothes. He liked me too! What did I know? Men are bastards! Do you hear me? I know all about polite conversation. I erased my Italian accent, and there's no garlic in my food. But once you dig below the surface, a woman is cornered. *Where is pleasure to be found?*

10: Rose

Peggy talks too much at breakfast: "I'm in the process of becoming tall and thin and blonde and Swedish; so I got this dog. People are supposed to look like their dogs, right? Who's to say he's not a Swedish terrier? This is America. A mongrel doesn't stay that way long. Positive thinking can go anywhere once you start!"

I digested that one along with my scrambled eggs and decaf. Peggy worries me. We met today in the Progresso section of the Kroger's in Grosse Pointe. I had never seen so many brands of Italian food, and she was in a big hurry after she picked the wrong can and the whole display collapsed. She grabbed a half-price sale sign and stuck it on the bent cans. I need someone who keeps her head in a crisis. "Don't dye your hair," I said. "Aerobics is no answer," I added.

Last night I dreamed I was on a bus, and the driver was my first psychiatrist. We were on our way to his funeral, and we were deciding if it was appropriate for me to be there. The bus stopped and the door opened. I was on my own.

There used to be rules in therapy. "You need a good reason to break them," he said. He broke two. He came to my wedding. A sure stamp of approval. He visited me every week after he slapped me in the hospital for making love to a bottle of Thorazine. That place had rules too —no private doctor. He came anyway, and he called me "Rose" for three months. After that it was Mrs. Sullivan all the way. "This hospital will teach you patience," he said, as he walked with me between the redbrick buildings. It was snowing, and the drifts were high. He wore big galoshes with the snaps unbuckled. I learned that lesson. I waited ten years to have babies. I wanted to be sure I had what it took: my brains straight, a bedroom for each one, nothing fancy. What I hadn't bargained for was my children.

They were like that from the beginning, but nobody figured it out until they hit nursery school. Now I'm patient every day. But there's only so far you can travel on patience and wisecracks, which brings me back to Peggy. Her husband just left her for a frail woman whose breasts will never sag. She looks great in clothes, and that's the only part of her that's flat. Peggy is a little too voluptuous, and she grayed early.

I felt like screaming by the time the coffee was cold, so I can't give Peggy any of that cheap advice about making your own silver lining out of papier-mâché. I keep in mind what my doctor said about breaking rules. Tall and Swedish, my foot! "Tell your cousins about that flat-chested bitch!" I said. She grinned. She has three, and they work on the dock and live in St. Clair Shores. Fights were a lot easier in the fifth grade on the playground. A little bloody. But the school nurse took care of that, and we thought the nuns knew it all.

11: Rose

I've told Peggy more than once that you have to be content with a little philosophy after you've laughed yourself into a frenzy. I know a few stories that aren't funny. But I thought they were. For years.

When you have kids, it's heat and ice and, sometimes, pure joy. Long and short spells of each. Or just a flash. You never know what's coming and, after a point, there's not much you can do. Either it will or it won't . . . happen. Either you will or you won't . . . sleep. Fill in your own blanks. You won't find this approach in a textbook, because it is no solution. *It's all you have left of what you started out with.*

I hate to sound vague, but I don't like to talk about my family. I like to nail down my pleasures and lock the door. When I can find him, my husband touches my hand and says a few words: "We're out of razors, Rose, and, while you're at it, get me some mouthwash!" I don't pay attention to his directions anymore. "It's Sunday," I tally up the week for him. "What the hell does that have to do

with it?" My hand is on the volume, and I turn it loud
enough to make a difference. Music has its place.

I was fiddling with the maps Peggy brought back from
Boston when I thought about taking a week off, myself.
You can be sure I wouldn't go that far or hole up with a
stack of books, even if it did rain. And I hate museums.
All those bloodless women doing something cultural and
tiptoeing through the hollow rooms. That leaves the
streets. Watching and walking. And new rooms, away
from this house. San Antonio wouldn't be bad. They
speak Spanish down there, and it's like a foreign country. On the water.

Nothing is happening here. The high school principal
gained ten pounds and quit running. I walk the track
with my tapes, and now nobody stops me to talk. And I'm
never going to pay my library fines. Let them look for me!

12: Peggy

"Rose, I'll tell you the truth. It's one of three things: a bad
face-lift, a cut throat, or a new type of cerebral palsy." We
are sitting on the big porch of the Grand Hotel at Macki-
naw Island. The woman with the strange expression didn't
stay long, but it was obviously a hacked-up face-lift. I just
couldn't resist a little specificity. It's not easy getting a
laugh out of Rose anymore, and we aren't getting any
younger.

Rose is seeing a shrink again, and he told her to take
vacations. "If you can't change something, get the hell
away from it." A little common sense helps, and so does
the medicine he gave her. She dies if she eats a piece of
cheese or takes a drink, so she is, as they say, on the
wagon. "See, I finally get you the silver flask, and you
give out on me!" Rose mumbled something about San
Antonio.

I saw the shrink near the music shell at Meadowbrook,
climbing the hill with a picnic basket: white hair and red
face and a blustery laugh that speaks to me. Beethoven

took a backseat for a minute. He shook my hand and smiled at Rose.

"Civilized," I'll say that for him. I'm not into sabotage, so she and I are planning a few more vacations. Who knows what we will find? We have nothing to lose.

I even bought some new clothes. I'm sick of black and, anyway, summer is here and it's time to lighten up a little.

13: Rose

My husband John is a practical man. He can't pass up a sale on hubcaps, and he has no feel for the weather. It is a fall afternoon. I'm sitting in the car waiting for the walk he promised me and remembering Sundays when we were first married, when we walked through Ann Arbor and ate sauerbraten at the Old German. The Michigan campus was beautiful, and the woods were private and rough.

These days I'd settle for kicking up leaves on a street with tract homes. I dream of torching automobiles. They do that now in Detroit. But the cars have to be from Germany or Japan. In my dreams, it is always our car. The flames stretch and curl around the door handles. The light is blinding, and I wake up in relief. Dreams are only make-believe, in spite of what my shrink says. Most of the time you forget them by the time the teakettle whistles.

I was killing time in a mall the following Monday when I caught a sale of framed photographs. They were big and the subjects predictable.

I was drawn to the cars: gull-winged coupes, a 300 SL with the doors up, a red Ferrari seen from the oddest angle. The cars had a shine that pulled me right in. I bought the red Ferrari. I can never decide what to eat in those places with open seating and wall after wall of choices, so I went home and opened a Stroh's.

Before I met my husband, I had a job as a librarian at Jam Handy's on Grand Boulevard. The company made movies. Movies of cars. In Detroit, the wheel is everything and everywhere. Summer was a slow season because new models came out in September. Then you had to have files at your fingertips and be prepared to send out for lunch and work past seven. The men in the office had all fled high school English for public relations. They weren't sorry, and they stuck together. I was the only woman. Nobody mentioned cars in the off hours.

After work in the summers, we took the bus to the Brass Rail and ordered up. The glasses were big and frosty, and the waiters didn't push you around. Working women wore white shoes and carried gloves till Labor Day. When Walter Reuther got up to speak, you knew summer was over.

That September we walked all the way from the General Motors building up Cass Avenue to hear Herb Gold. When you've had a few, exercise seems a natural thing.

I just knew we would leave the city and never mention taillights again. It seemed a sure thing. But we didn't. Jam Handy died. Even swimming laps at seventy-five and Christian Science can't save you! The men ended up in the PR department at Ford. The first one laid the way for the rest. I got married. That's no answer, but in those days it was.

Let's skip the diapers and the PTA. I did all the things I said I never would. But I didn't feel at home with all that money and the Bloomfield Hills crowd. Which brings me back to Sunday and the walk.

I have a few questions. Now that the kids are gone, why doesn't romance fill the corners? We don't have to lock the bedroom door or set the alarm for the middle of the night. And why is it so hard to take a walk on Sunday afternoon? Here I sit looking at that red Ferrari and wondering where the odd angle would look best.

Did you know Herb Gold moved to California? My brother, who carries a beeper and takes care of computers, got transferred out there. Gold is still writing novels, and his hair has turned white. That Ferrari is frozen in glass and the red matches my rug, but my husband can't figure out why I bought it.

14: Peggy

Elisa visits me, but I never ask her about what goes on over there. Harvey told me he wanted a hostess, and it's obvious he could stand a little time-out from the bedroom. How could I be jealous? It's not a life I wanted. I grew up with it. Entertaining? Harvey entertained me in the bath-tub. He entertained me on the back porch when the stars were out.

Men are such fools. I would have been content with his decline. But loyalty wasn't in his vocabulary. Was it deeper than that? What does middle age mean? I'm waiting here in my Eames chair trying to concentrate on my books, but all I see is Rose's face. Her chin sags, and she needs a haircut. Her picture isn't here. I don't keep pictures in this room.

My father died last week, and I didn't go to the funeral. My mother will never get over it, and my brothers got nasty. I just couldn't listen to all those lies and watch his partner use the time to his best advantage. I haven't been inside a church in ten years, and I don't know what that kind of respect means. Respect for the dead? What is it?

I have been reading a biography of Diane Arbus this week, and I think I see what she was after. You can get caught up in her psychology, but I prefer to concentrate on the photographs: the fashion, the freaks, the faces, the grainy backgrounds, the horror in some, and the part that doesn't fit into words in most. Once you get in that place and see it, you are surrounded by mysteries, and it takes a lot of energy to chase them around in your head. There is no time-out for dead rituals or dead men who saw the horror early on and became a part of it.

15: Rose

No matter what Peggy says, I know fashion is meaningless, but I believe in covering up. Loose is best. I have time now to think about details. So I made a plan and stuck to it. Pink. Everything matches, and it all goes in the washer and comes out wrinkled. That's the look this summer. I topped it off with some boots that make people stop me and ask where I got them. My husband calls me his elf. I don't know what I am or what I'm hiding, but I feel safe in my new clothes. Peggy calls me "Pinky." The children are gone.

We were eating lunch at a cafeteria yesterday when Peggy lit a cigarette and told me about a new vacation spot. She has gone overboard on the advice my shrink gave me. I don't need to get away anymore, but Peggy is bullheaded.

I take my medicine and listen to her ramble.

On Friday morning I see my doctor and report on the week. By the time the hour is over, I have ruined my manicure and developed a full-blown sneezing attack. It's hard to breathe with all that stale air and the diplomas and awards on the wall. His wife arranges the flowers and they change every week, and his chair creaks and slides on its casters. Sometimes he even gets mad, and his face turns redder. He calls it irritated. I wait. I've considered a few alternatives, but such drama seems pointless.

I didn't know what it would be like without the children. I leave his office and go to my exercise class. I watch the mirror and the other people in it. Music fills the room, and I know I'll be late if I don't hurry. The ride home is full of stoplights.

There are some things you can't talk about. How did I get this far without screaming in the streets? And what comes next? The gardener is planting a tea olive outside our bedroom window, and the maid is never late.

"You're out of razors, Mrs. Sullivan!"

She doesn't understand why I laugh.